One Thing That's True

CHERYL FOGGO

Kids Can Press Ltd.

First U.S. edition 1998

We acknowledge the support of the Canada Council for the Arts and the Ontario Arts Council for our publishing program.

Published in Canada by
Kids Can Press Ltd.
29 Birch Avenue
Toronto, ON M4V 1E2

Published in the U.S. by
Kids Can Press Ltd.
85 River Rock Drive, Suite 202
Buffalo, NY 14207

Edited by Charis Wahl
Interior designed by Tom Dart/First Folio Resource Group, Inc.
Printed and bound in Canada

97 0 9 8 7 6 5 4 3 2 1

Canadian Cataloguing in Publication Data

Foggo, Cheryl
One thing that's true

ISBN 1-55074-411-9

I. Title.

PS8561.0385053 1997 jC813'.54 C97-930959-X
PZ7.F63On 1997

ACKNOWLEDGMENTS

I would like to thank the following people for their intelligent and encouraging remarks about Roxanne's story: Clem Martini, Chandra Martini, Rebecca Shaw, Rochelle Lamoureux, Megan Hardisty, Darcy Foggo, Dion Foggo, Richard Foggo, Noel Foggo-Lamoureux, Pauline Foggo and Pearl Hayes. I would also like to thank Larry Lamoureux, Vicky Burton and Eera Jadav for helping with the little research details that matter a lot. I must also pay tribute to Otis Redding, Ray Charles, James Brown, Esther Phillips, Mahalia Jackson and a host of other R and B, jazz and gospel musicians for making music that's good for people to listen to while writing. And I would especially like to thank my editor, Charis Wahl, for having a crush on Michael. I also thank The Canada Council for their generous assistance.

To Clem, for reading this manuscript eight thousand times without losing interest.

And to Chandra and Miranda, for filling my house with the best times.

June

CHAPTER 1

I WAS AT HOME, IN THE ATTIC, LYING ON THOSE OLD, FLAT futons Joel and I had dragged up there. I looked out the window, not thinking about anything at all except the paint cracking on the windowsill when I noticed Orion's stars were white. There was no color. No red, green, purple, blue, gold and silver like in the pictures I used to draw. They were just white. I thought maybe it was the window, it's round and a little bit tinted, maybe it was distorting the color of the stars. I was down the ladder in about three seconds and out the front door on the deck. I looked up, and saw it really was true.

I felt different. Like my life was about to change.

The next day in English class, Mrs. Verdecchio asked me to read my homework aloud. I had the pages in front of me, but there was nothing on them, so I winged it. "Roxanne means 'dawn,' Camille means 'handmaiden,' Jacob means 'he who supplants,'" I faked, then I sat down.

Mrs. Verdecchio said, "Yes?"

I said, "That's all."

She scratched the tip of her nose, then asked, "Did you understand the assignment?"

I understood the assignment. I just didn't understand why it was any business of hers why my parents named me what they named me. I didn't say that. I just nodded and sat down.

Mrs. Verdecchio said, "You can do better than that. Hand it in tomorrow. There's a late penalty of ten percent."

I shrugged and said I'd take the zero, and she looked like her whole world had crashed.

A small part of me felt sorry for her because she had great passion for teaching and was always trying to get us excited, but it never worked. I felt a bit sorry that everyone hated her, not because she was old, like she thought, but because she was crazy. Everyone hated the way she couldn't remember names. We hated the way she started out talking quiet and sweet, like "I want for you TONY CUMMINGS to quiet down!" shrieking the name in the middle, with spit flying from the corner of her mouth. We hated it that Tony's name was actually Cunningham and no matter how many times he gritted his teeth and told her that, she never remembered. We hated it when she called Bobby Arthur, Arthur, thinking it was his first name. No one cared about Robbie Burns, or was impressed when she tried to roll the "R" to sound Scottish.

Still, in a small way, I felt sorry that I had been one of her favorite students and that a lot of people hated her, and that she must have been thinking then that I hated her too.

I thought about her being alone in her house, maybe later that night, making tea just for herself because her husband had died two years before, alone making tea and not having very many more years to live and not much to live for because of the way her students felt about her and part of me wanted to cry.

But some people in the class looked at me differently because I'd said I'd take a low mark. They were thinking, you're one of us now, you're cool, and even though I didn't respect those people, I enjoyed having them look at me that way.

And I kept enjoying it until I was leaving to go home for the afternoon and I saw Mr. Morgan getting a drink at the fountain. Normally he would have stopped to talk, but he just wiped his chin and walked right by. I wondered if he'd heard that I'd been mean to Mrs. Verdecchio. I wondered if you had to be liked by all the teachers or none.

Anyway, Tuesday at lunchtime Laura Pinkerton and I went over to the high school to meet Joel and his friends behind the bike racks, just like always. Except it wasn't like always, because Kyle Kroeger was there. He was trying to get attention by punching the guys on the arms and flirting with Laura, and when that failed he turned on me.

"This isn't a lunchtime day care," he sneered. I ignored him, but he kept at it. "Hey, Joel, you still playing house with your little sister?"

At first I couldn't think what he meant, then I realized he was referring to a game Joel and I used to play about being two kids named Tommy and Susie who had bad parents and had to run away from Calgary to survive on their own in the wilderness.

Kyle had a look to him, the look of people who are untalented, unwanted, unattractive, without a future and want to go around breaking things.

I didn't want those flat eyes on me, so I asked him, "Doesn't your mother ever tell you to wash your face?"

I guess he didn't want to answer my question, because he reached out for me, grabbed my shirt, pulled it out of my jeans and tried to shove his hand under it. I smacked him in the eye with the back of my hand, but not in time to keep him from squeezing the place where my breasts would have been if I'd had any.

It all happened really fast. Before I could say anything, Joel was punching him in the face and swearing and trying to kick him in the head. Michael Barron grabbed Joel, but by that time Kyle was curled up on the ground. He got up and went into the school, bent over, holding a handful of blood under his nose. The rest of us stood there, looking at each other.

The principal's office had a familiar feel to it, even though I'd never been there before. I started thinking I was having one of those parallel-time/out-of-body experiences when it occurred to me that things looked familiar only because Joel had described them to me.

I remember thinking, "Great, now I'm starting to share Joel's memories."

Mr. Wagner called my and Laura's principal, Mr. Toth, and everyone's parents, to a meeting in his office.

Dad's lips are too big to actually draw them into a straight line, but they were pretty tight. He was mad about taking time off work and really mad about my recent encounter with the zero in Mrs. Verdecchio's class. I was mad too – at her for telling.

Mr. Wagner was droning on about violence and fighting and zero tolerance. He said Joel was right to intervene, but he had stepped over the line from intervention to revenge.

"You know what'll happen if the press gets wind of this," he said, and my mother didn't miss a beat.

"They'll turn it into something racial."

Her greatest fear is that everything is racial, or will be perceived as racial or will start a race war and everyone in the world will be killed. She was probably thinking Mr. Wagner was thinking Black parents are irresponsible and don't know how to make their children behave, which I don't think he was because the person he was really burned at was Kyle Kroeger.

He told Laura and me to stay off Silver Heights' schoolgrounds until we're students there next year. He gave Joel a very stern warning and sent him to Mrs.

Gledahill for anger-management counseling. Kyle, he suspended.

Kyle's father went crazy.

"My kid is the only one who got hurt! He's sitting here with his nose puffed out like a mushroom and he gets suspended?"

Mr. Wagner got all red and sweaty and finally interrupted Mr. Kroeger's tirade.

"Let me say something to you, sir. You're lucky I don't expel him altogether. You'll be lucky if this girl's parents don't call the police. I suggest you do some work with him over the summer – one more time this year or next, he's gone."

The Kroegers and Kyle slunk out, sullen. Kyle's father had the same dead look in his eyes as Kyle, and seeing them both together made my spine a little cold. They didn't tell him to apologize to me.

As soon as we were out of the school where no one could hear us, Mom started to cry and got in Joel's face.

"Haven't I told you about fighting? Haven't I told you? Beating people up is not the answer to anything. That's for a different kind of people. We don't do that."

Dad looked at Mom like she was crazy. "What was he s'posed to do? Stand there and let that jackass manhandle his sister?"

"You watch your language, Willis. I won't have that in front of the children. This is for the police, not Joel, to settle."

"No! Don't phone the police!" Everyone looked at me when I burst out like that, and when I started crying, Joel stomped off to the van, like always, hating my crying.

"Okay everybody, calm down here. Let's not let this get out of hand." Dad put his arm around Mom and she collapsed into his shoulder, weeping even more.

"Take a breath, honey," he said.

It was chaos. You'd have thought someone had just died.

CHAPTER 2

THINGS WERE INTENSE FOR A COUPLE OF DAYS. JOEL was grounded and they made me spend a whole Saturday finishing the "names and their meanings" assignment.

The next day, Mom was going to church alone again. I heard her ask Dad to go, like always, and he said no, like always, that he had to go by the office and do some work. I felt sorry for her and kinda sorta thought I should go, but I didn't want to leave Joel alone due to his weird mood, so I told her maybe next time.

I hadn't been to church in a while and I missed some of the smells. I missed the dusty-paper smell of the hymnbooks, the peppermint from Mrs. Bagley's breath floating over my shoulder, and Uncle Lee's cologne. Mostly, I missed the smell of the pine benches. I missed imagining what the actual trees must have smelled like, if twenty-year-old benches could remind me of some long ago forest that I'd never seen.

As soon as Mom and Dad were both gone, Joel asked me to go to the bird sanctuary with him.

"You're grounded, jerk."

"So?"

It was a kind of beginning. It was the worst thing he'd ever asked me to do.

I stood in the kitchen for five minutes, thinking about how Joel and I had done everything together all our lives, and how he was now wanting to do some things I didn't want to do. I thought about what his face looked like when he was pounding Kyle, and I got a sick feeling inside me. I started imagining him on the C-train without me and maybe sitting across from some skinheads and getting that look on his face again and getting into a fight. I thought about how unhappy he'd seemed lately and how birding always seemed to help.

I opened my mouth and out came, "Do we have time to get back before them?"

As soon as I asked, he knew I was going with him. He grinned and tried to cuff me on the head, but I blocked his arm and whirled around, giving him a fake, feeble karate kick to the gut.

It was a long ride on the train and bus to the sanctuary, but we didn't mind, it was a peaceful thing. We found the emptiest train car and sat across from each other, staring out the window, collecting our thoughts. We didn't talk much. There were no skinheads.

There's a huge poplar not far from the footbridge at the sanctuary. Many times we'd crawled up in there, right out onto some of the big branches that hang over the river. We'd look down over the fish and the ducks and the geese.

Joel used to study birds with Uncle Lee, who was always bringing over feeders and books. Then he figured out that Uncle Lee wasn't really interested in birds, he was just trying to deprogram Joel. He was always saying we should be doing things we haven't been "conditioned" to do, which for some reason led him to bird-watching. He and Dad would argue all the time, because Dad likes sports and has a huge collection of jazz albums and Uncle Lee thought this was bad for us.

"Not gonna tell 'em they can't play basketball 'cause they're Black, Lee."

"Just encourage them in other areas."

"Why? Nothin' to be ashamed of."

These arguments would always make me wonder what happened to Mom and Uncle Lee when they were growing up, that they both got so obsessed with this image thing. Grandma and Grandpa seemed so normal.

Anyway, Dad would really go on about it, just to get a rise out of Uncle Lee. And Uncle Lee fell for it every time. They both just wanted us to be happy – basketball or tennis or trumpet or harp. Or bird-watching. Whatever. But neither of them ever tried to understand the other. They just liked to argue.

So, Joel had decided it was phony for Uncle Lee to pretend to like birds. He told Uncle Lee he'd lost interest, when really he was still kind of a fanatic and liked to point out creatures, which to me just looked like regular sparrows, and tell me they were dark-eyed juncos.

That's what I was thinking about while we were in the tree. That, and about how embarrassing it was to have

Michael there when Kyle put his stupid hands up my shirt.

All the way home, I was wondering if God thinks it's wrong for a person to sneak behind her parents' backs and sort of lie to them, even if she's not doing it for herself, she's doing it to help someone. I just had to look at Joel to know it was better for him to spend the morning at the bird sanctuary than it would have been to stay home brooding. Then I started wondering suppose there is no God, where do your thoughts about God go and what do they mean? Then I started thinking about thoughts and ideas in general and where do they go. Like if you like someone and they don't know it, if you think about them enough, do those thoughts penetrate their consciousness. Then I started thinking about Michael Barron and the look of horror in his eyes when he was pinning Joel's arms to keep him from killing Kyle, and asking me if I was okay. From there I went on to remember the time I saw Michael in the gym at the community center playing basketball without his shirt on. I got really embarrassed by my thoughts at that point, so I went back to thinking that I had actually done a good thing by going to the bird sanctuary with my brother. And those warm thoughts about my wisdom lasted until we turned the corner onto our street and saw Dad pulling his car into the garage.

CHAPTER 3

RIGHT THEN I KNEW, NO QUESTION, DAD AND MOM would find nothing funny, wise or cute about us going out when Joel was grounded.

We looked at each other. He grabbed my arm and pulled me back behind Mrs. Chisholm's fence. My heart was pounding. "Let's go this way," I said. "My bedroom window is open."

We don't have an alley behind our house, just a concrete trench sort of thing that runs between our street's backyards and the backyards across from us. I thought we could stay low and creep between the fences and somehow get into the house before Dad realized we weren't there. Luckily, our gate was unlocked, because the lock is very high up and awkward to reach from the outside. We got into the yard and grabbed the ladder from the side of the house and had it propped up underneath my window before looking up and seeing it was closed. Then I remembered closing it because the wind had blown a photo of me and Grandma off the dresser.

We could hear Dad calling us from the bottom of the steps in the living room.

"Come on!" Joel hissed. He pulled me by my sleeve over to the tree, shoved me down on the swing and started pushing me, like he used to do about a hundred years ago.

"Dad!" he shouted. "Dad? We're out here."

The patio doors opened and Dad stepped out in his bare feet. He stood staring at us. I suddenly burst out into giddy laughter, partly because I had those little tears you get when you've just missed some sort of big trouble, but also because I thought we must look ridiculous and Dad wasn't going to buy it.

Funny though. He didn't seem to think anything at all about us being in the backyard on the swing. He seemed preoccupied and sad. Joel whispered something I couldn't quite hear, but it sounded like "I wonder where *he's* been?"

"There you are," Dad said. He turned to go back in, then mumbled over his shoulder. "Don't push too high, son."

That's what he used to say when I was five and Joel was six.

And I can't help but think everything probably would have been different if Joel had not skipped school the next day.

We left the house and walked all the way together, so I didn't find out what he had done until I got home at four o'clock.

Wagner called Mom, found out she thought Joel was at school, and handed down a three-day suspension. When Joel showed up at about 6:30, Dad and Mom were arguing. Mom accused Dad of "tacitly" approving of Joel's fighting and not supporting her. Dad asked Joel what he thought he was doing, skipping out of school, and Joel's great response was, "I don't think I owe you any answers."

I felt like saying, "There you go, Joel, that'll really patch things up." Dad grounded Joel again. I felt like saying, "Yeah, that's really working Dad."

He also took away Joel's learner's license and driving privileges indefinitely.

Joel stomped off, while Mom and Dad continued bickering. I drifted outside. Then I got bored, so I went back in for the phone. I called Laura and we talked about how dumb families can be.

CHAPTER 4

JOEL SPENT THE NEXT DAY IN THE ATTIC WITH THE trapdoor closed. Mom had the house looking like an operating room, due to her habit of cleaning like a maniac whenever she's worried about something. I thought of saying, "Hey, relax, Mom. When I'm depressed, I just lie around in the attic listening to depressing music, which makes me feel like I might as well kill myself." But I didn't.

Anyway, that particular day, Laura and I shot baskets at lunchtime, on our own schoolground. It felt strange. Everyone at our school had decided we were snobby for hanging with older people, so no one would talk with us or shoot hoops. I said to Laura, "So what?" It had become my stock answer for everything, "so what," a very good pair of words that conveys the truth of life.

Laura told me that day she thought Michael Barron liked me.

"Yes, Laura," I said. "The best-looking guy about to go into grade ten is going to be interested in a thirteen-year-old stick."

She pointed out that whenever we went over to the high school, he only talked to me, that he never even looked at her. *I* pointed out it was because I'm Joel's sister, but she said, "Nah."

To be honest, I had noticed that Michael didn't seem to be interested in Laura. Normally I couldn't get any attention when she was around. Even the teachers, the creepy ones I mean, ogled her.

She has long, dark-honey-colored hair that curls and great skin *and* green eyes. Not just green eyes the way people think of green eyes. More the color of emeralds than the sea.

Sometimes when I looked at myself in the old mirror that hangs next to the chest in the attic, I would compare myself to Laura. I would tell myself, that mirror distorts, and that I didn't really look like the image I saw peeping back. Either it was the mirror, or I was one of the ugliest people alive.

At least I was better than her at sports.

While she tried to perfect her jump shot, I got the idea to invite Uncle Lee and his girlfriend Sarah over on the weekend and cook dinner for everyone. I decided I'd make a great big pot of button-bone spare ribs, along with other recipes I've been getting from Grandma, and call it history or tradition night; sweet night. Knowing there was nothing that cheered my family up like good food, I thought I was brilliant.

Yeah.

CHAPTER 5

IT RAINED THE DAY BEFORE MY DINNER AND WAS DRAB; I heard on the radio it was the rainiest June since 1910. But the weather didn't seem to be getting anyone down.

Joel was acting normal. Not normal as in regular. But he was acting normal for Joel. He was making his dumb rhymes and playing his imaginary basketball game, dribbling and shooting, also boxing his formidable air opponent and punting an invisible football. Mom let him drive her to the mall in the afternoon, but told him not to tell Dad. I remember thinking what a bizarre couple of people I have for parents. She got mad at Dad for not backing her up, and practically forced him to ground Joel, then she undermined Dad and swore Joel to secrecy. It was almost as if she wanted to help him, as if she knew what was going to happen.

I spent most of the day planning and preparing the dinner, and thinking about stuff I should work on, like my left brain. Math. Science. Uncle Lee was always saying I should be thinking about a career in the sciences, because I'm a girl and the future needs me. I was thinking I shouldn't slack off on the left brain just because I have an overdeveloped right brain. I had read that even geniuses use only about 12 percent of their brain's capacity. What if I could get up to 15 percent? I was fantasizing about how everyone would admire me and how that would be good.

I phoned Uncle Lee to make sure he and Sarah could come and he talked to me about the rain and how it used to rain all the time in Vancouver when he lived there. Also I phoned Grandma, to check a few details on some of her recipes. My menu was button bones, wild rice, corn, sweet potatoes, toasted-almond-and-mandarin-orange salad and raspberry pie for dessert. Grandma told me she would be coming down to the city the next week to shop. She also said not to beat the eggs too stiffly for my pie. She said button bone spareribs used to be slave food, food that the slave owners wouldn't eat, and that her recipe came down through many generations of her family. She was very pleased that I had taken an interest in her recipes and her old stories.

Then something strange happened. She asked me how I'd been doing and I started telling her about the mini track meet we'd had at school on Friday. I told her how muddy and slippery it was and that Ralphie Schampf had slipped and fallen in the long-jump pit, getting himself completely covered in mud. I was one second away from crying, so I told Grandma I had to go. I hung up the phone, then raced up the stairs, trying to get to the attic before anyone could see me crying. Mom was in the kitchen unloading the dishwasher. She followed me when I ran past, she followed me right up the ladder and knocked on the panel, asking if I was okay. I said I was, she knew I wasn't, but I didn't open the door, so she went away. I heard her sigh.

The attic window sometimes sticks, but I pushed hard and got it open. I stuck my arm out to check the temperature of the rain, which was warm.

I couldn't get the picture of Ralphie tripping over the foul board out of my mind, and everyone laughing at him like they always do because he's overweight and clumsy.

And that made me think about the first time I saw Michael. I was in grade two and really shy and had a bit of an English accent, because we'd spent the year before living in London. Being embarrassed about my accent made me not want to talk to anyone, even though I wanted to tell people to stop picking on Ralphie. Michael was in grade three. One day he saw the Kroegers and some others tormenting Ralphie, and Michael yelled at them and helped Ralphie pick up his backpack and library books and walked him home. Even though I didn't know then that he would grow up to be beautiful and a great athlete and everything else he is, I knew he was a really good person.

So with my arm out the window, I sat there feeling lousy. I should have taken it as an omen.

CHAPTER 6

THINGS STARTED OUT OKAY. UNCLE LEE AND SARAH were both in good moods when they arrived, and Mom was practically hopping, she was so proud of me. She got out her good china and crystal, and the lace tablecloth she got from her grandmother. I left the rice on a little too long and it burned and stuck to the pot, so I had to start over again, but other than that everything was perfect. Just like I thought, eating well seemed to lift the gloom. I did hear Sarah asking Mom about the thing with Kyle Kroeger and Mom whispered something back, but they stopped when I banged a few pots around. After that, the conversation stayed pretty safe. Even Dad and Uncle Lee were being civil to each other. There wasn't one grain of rice left over at the end and I was feeling great.

After the main course was finished, Uncle and I cleared the table while Mom made coffee. Dad put on some Ray Charles and Joel sat in the living room talking to Sarah.

Joel told her he was looking forward to getting back to school on Monday, that his week had been really boring. Without turning around, Dad said, "You'll be going to school in the afternoon, but you've got an appointment in the morning."

"An appointment for what?"

"A doctor's appointment."

"For what?"

At that point we all went to the living room. Mom was staring at Dad, she didn't take her eyes off him. Then she said, "Are you crazy, Willis? Why would you choose this moment?"

Joel asked, "For what?"

She put her hand on his arm. "Son, we think you need … help. We've made an appointment with a counselor."

"You mean a psychiatrist?"

There was silence, except for the heart banging in my chest.

Joel and I'd had lots of talks. We spent half our time talking about Mom and Dad, and lately he'd been saying, over and over, that they didn't like him. And I always said he was crazy. And until that moment, I really thought he was.

And maybe I could have gone on convincing myself that there was some good reason for what they had done, if they had acted like it. But instead, they got defensive.

Uncle Lee flipped out. He was shaking. "Are you trying to destroy this boy, Willis? Whose idea was this?"

"We both agreed on it, Lee," Mom interrupted. "We

need help. We don't know what to do anymore." Then she looked at Dad again. "But this was not the time. Roxanne has worked so hard to make this nice ..."

"I'm not going to a shrink." Joel calmly picked up his coat and left the house.

Dad said, "We had to tell him sometime. What, was I supposed to spring it on him Monday morning while he brushed his teeth? I thought it would be better for him to have everyone around ..."

"That child no more needs a psychiatrist than I do, Helen," said Uncle Lee. "Don't put your problems with Willis on his shoulders."

The look on Mom's face added new meaning to the word "distraught." "She's not a psychiatrist, she's a psychologist. You're making it seem worse than it is. You'll make Joel think there's some kind of stigma ..."

Sarah went over to put her arms around her.

"You're the ones that are crazy," I said, but no one paid any attention.

Dad told Uncle Lee it was none of his business. I think he felt backed into a corner and that's why he was being so nasty.

"He *is* my business. And I'm watching out for him. I'm watching you. Let's go, Sarah."

They got their coats from the closet and slammed out the door.

My pie was still sitting in the fridge.

I went to my room and lay down on my bed and hugged the stuffing out of Bunny.

I must have dozed a little. At one point I heard the van starting in the garage and knew Dad was going out to look for Joel. Then a while later I heard Mom climb the stairs to their room. About two hours after that, I heard the door open. I heard Dad call out softly, "Son?" but Joel didn't answer him. He came up the stairs and knocked on my door. We went up to the attic.

He'd been walking down by the twin bridges. He said it wasn't even completely dark down there yet.

He seemed relieved that I was angry about what they were trying to do to him. I guess I'd been calling him crazy so much, he was starting to wonder if that was what I really thought.

I had to be careful about what I said. It wasn't the usual situation where you complain about your parents making you do something, even though deep inside you know they're right. I was just as confused as Joel. Why were they acting that way?

He insisted he wasn't going to see any shrink on Monday, that he'd run away first. I told him I thought that would just play into their image of him being out of control. I said it was like when you're a little kid and you say you're going to take off. Not real. I reminded Joel he still had his dignity and could show them up with that. Show them that they couldn't scare him into acting crazy.

And he answered, "At our age, the only thing you have

that's really yours is your thoughts. Everything else, someone bought for you or gave you. That's why they have so much control over us. Now they're trying to make me give my thoughts away."

We crept downstairs to get the pie and saw that Mom had left the coffee pot on, so we took some coffee too. I'd never had coffee before. It wasn't too bad with a lot of milk and sugar.

Back in the attic, Joel told me he had dropped in at Dad's office about a month before and had seen him with a blond woman. They weren't doing anything, but Joel said it didn't look like business. Dad was sitting at his desk with his feet up and a drink in his hand. And this woman was sitting across from him, with *her* feet up and a drink in *her* hand. Dad jumped up really quickly, very nervously and introduced Joel to this Cynthia, who smiled at him and said, "So you're Joel."

Since then, Dad had been pretending it didn't happen.

"Maybe he's having an affair," Joel said. "Maybe he's trying to scare me because I know what he's up to."

At first I said, no way. No way would Dad have an affair, first of all, and no way would he do something mean to Joel to cover up something *he* had done.

But I had to admit I didn't have the answers.

Anyway, I finally knew why Joel had been pushing Dad's buttons. He thought our father was cheating on our mother and he thought Mom knew about it. I was sure he was wrong about the Mom-knowing part. If something *was* going on and my mother found out about it, Dad would be dead, along with Cynthia. We'd be the children left behind while our mother went to prison for a double murder.

After we had devoured the entire pie, Joel fell asleep on some of the cushions. I covered him with a blanket, then sat for a long time looking out the window at the apple tree and the swing in the moonlight. The tree was covered in blossoms. I knew if I opened the window I'd be able to smell them, but I didn't want to. I thought their sweetness might break my heart.

I felt like I'd been swimming for a long time and couldn't feel the bottom and couldn't see the shore. I felt like I had gone somewhere and didn't know how to get home.

CHAPTER 7

THE NEXT DAY WAS LIKE ONE OF THOSE DREAMS WHERE you're floating, from one image to the next. You're living an ordinary life, doing things like tying your shoes and cleaning your sunglasses, waiting for something to happen. You're bored, but you're also aware that the boredom could easily be replaced by something worse, that would make you wish you could go back to being bored again.

That night Joel told Mom and Dad he would go to the appointment, not because he thought it would do any good, but because he felt he had no choice. He said if his own parents thought he was crazy there was nothing he could do about it. He looked very dignified while he was speaking, but also very skinny and vulnerable.

Of course they climbed all over each other to assure him they didn't think he was crazy, just "troubled."

Mom said, "When a child of your intelligence and potential starts making choices that could land him on the wrong path, it's time for the parents to take action."

And Joel directed his reply right at Dad. "Yeah, well

maybe you should take action on yourselves."

I thought Dad might get on Joel after that comment, but sometimes parents open their mouths and say just the opposite of what you're expecting, and at that moment Dad said, "Why don't you kids go on out tonight?"

"Hello, Dad, Joel's grounded, remember?" I put in.

"We'll call it square."

We took off up the stairs, making plans to go over to the pool to meet some of our friends when Dad called me back.

"Have you finished that assignment for Mrs. Verdecchio?"

"Yeah, long time ago."

"Okay."

"Wanna see it?"

"No, I trust you."

That was just bluffing luck on my part. If Dad had read it, he wouldn't have been very happy.

Wendy Shaeffer was at the pool, flirting embarrassingly with Joel, and Dawn Cowling was there, wearing one of her teeny, tiny bathing suits, and *she* was flirting with Michael. Dawn's one of the girls who already had breasts back in grade five when we saw that film in Family Life class, that *Girl, You're a Woman Now* thing. Laura did too, but she didn't strut around after the film.

All the guys stared at Dawn's body when they thought no one was looking. I was wearing my usual one-piece suit in the hopes that it would disguise my lack of shape. I'm a better swimmer than any of them, but the whole group paid zero attention to my aquatic prowess.

Mom never liked it when we were with any group that included Dawn and Matthew Cowling. She said Mr. and Mrs. Cowling were "not our kind of people." Which was true. Especially Mr. Cowling. I'd heard stories about him hitting them and being a drunk. I'd even heard he beat Mrs. Cowling.

I was sort of hanging on the edge of the group, trying to laugh and feel like a part of the sexy babes crowd, but it didn't work, so I decided to practice my backstroke in the lane not right at the edge of the pool, but next to it. I was swimming along, eyes closed, when I suddenly felt a kind of prick on my leg. I stopped, glanced down and there was a little pinpoint of blood on the side of my calf. I looked around a bit but couldn't see anything, so I went back to swimming. I touched the end, flipped my turn to go back and there was Matthew Cowling. He popped up out of the water like he'd been waiting for me. His teeth were really yellow, when he grinned what I suppose was his version of a menancing grin.

"You better not testify against Kyle."

Then he dove back under the water, swimming away with those herky-jerky movements he has. He looked bad and I wanted to laugh. What was he talking about? I wondered if it was him that had pricked me, with a pin or something. I looked over to the other side of the pool and saw that Kyle Kroeger was there, waiting for Matthew. Matthew got out of the water and the two of them started walking slowly over to where Joel was standing with a couple of our friends.

"Joel!" I shouted, my voice sounding echoey and shrill. I was in such a hurry to get to Joel first when I got out that I stepped on Michael's foot. He said ouch, but I was in too much of a panic to respond.

"Kroeger's here." I was out of breath.

Joel looked up and saw them heading our way.

"So?"

"Let's go, okay?"

Then Matthew and Kyle reached us.

"Hear you're going to a shrink," Kyle said to Joel.

That was so unexpected. I shot Laura a hard look. I knew Joel hadn't told anyone and Laura was the only person I had told. From her look, though, I knew it couldn't have been her.

"Let's go," I said again.

"I'm not afraid of these goofs."

I was so glad when Michael spoke up.

"Don't waste your time, Joel. Let's go."

The lifeguards had sort of noticed something was up and were starting toward us, so probably nothing would have happened anyway. We showered quick and walked home silently. I don't know what Joel was thinking. I was wondering about how Kyle could have known about the shrink. I was also thinking about what Matthew had said to me in the pool, and about the prick on my leg. I didn't tell Joel about it, and when we got home, I didn't tell Mom or Dad.

CHAPTER 8

If Joel's description of the psychologist was truthful, the only conclusion a person could have drawn was that all cartoon character psychologists were modeled on her. He said she had thick glasses, a big nose, tiny pig eyes, rumpled clothing, messy hair, the whole bit.

They talked for about an hour before Mom and Dad were brought in and Joel was sent out. Then Joel was brought back in and Dr. Leavens asked them all how they thought she could help. Joel said it was one of those moments where no one knows what to say next because someone has just asked a really stupid question. There was a full minute of silence, before the doctor laughed and then she became quite normal and businesslike. She told Mom and Dad she thought she could help Joel, but only if Joel felt the need for it. She could understand their concerns, blah, blah, blah, but that many of Joel's behaviors are typical of boys his age. She said Joel struck her as intelligent and healthy, blah, blah, and with a little luck and understanding she was sure he would turn out all right.

She finished with, "I know it's difficult, I have an eighteen-year-old daughter. But try to cut him some slack."

So she said for Joel to think about whether he wanted to go back and talk some more. She told Mom and Dad to see how things went over the summer.

Mom and Dad thought the woman was nutty. Joel liked her.

I was actually a little jealous. I thought it might be fun to visit a pig-eyed psychologist. Especially if I wasn't crazy, like Joel wasn't.

Grandma and Grandpa arrived the next day, and the following Sunday I went to church with Mom and them. It meant so much to Grandma to have me along.

The congregation sang "Farther Along" about five times. Sometimes they'll do that. There's no plan or anything, they'll just sing a song over and over. "Farther Along" is not like most hymns, which are about worship, or forgiveness or rejoicing. It's the people talking to each other, "Cheer up, my brother, live in the sunshine" and all that. It's people telling other people to carry on, that everything will be all right.

I had given up on praying a while before that, out of a kind of embarrassment that God would think I was being fake. Because when I prayed silently, I'd think, "What's the point of this? God supposedly already knows my thoughts, so there's no need for me to organize my thoughts into a prayer." And when I prayed out loud, my voice sounded funny and I felt even sillier. But I'd been feeling so desperate about our family that I thought I'd try it out that day.

I apologized to God for not thinking of Him quite the way I used to, or the way Grandma and my Mom wanted me to. I told Him I was afraid of Him sometimes, afraid that He might really be that punishing kind of God some people believe gave AIDS to gays on purpose.

I admitted I wanted for there to be a God. A nice God to watch over me and take care of me and more or less keep the whole world in His hands. And my family.

After we got home I listened to music with Joel the rest of the afternoon.

We were on the floor in the den. I could hear Mom and Dad and Grandma and Grandpa and Uncle Lee and Sarah in the kitchen, laughing and talking, and my Mom sounding like a woman who trusted her husband.

But what did Joel see? What did he see? That was in my head.

When I was little, whenever we were up at my grandparents' farm, I used to stay awake at night as long as I could, to hear my grandmother singing. I loved the sound of her voice.

The next afternoon, I sat on the bed in the spare room while she was packing their things to go home. I asked her if she would teach me to drive when I turned fourteen. She said, "You can drive my car, you can borrow my clothes, you can wear my jewelry."

As if I'd borrow her clothes.

She said for me to look after my brother.

"He's older. Shouldn't he be looking after me?"

"Nothing to do with any of that. The one that's capable of doing the looking after, that's the one that has to do it."

So I said okay.

She asked me about the Kyle Kroeger incident. I felt my face get hot and little tears of embarrassment appeared in the corners of my eyes. I wanted to run right out of there and kill Mom on the spot.

"I don't want to talk about that, Gram."

"Why not?"

"Because it was nothing and people keep trying to make a big deal out of it."

"If it was nothing, why can't you talk about it?"

I got a little rank with her.

"I didn't say I *can't* talk about it, I said I don't want to."

She didn't respond to my rudeness.

"I've always told you about respect. You have a right to that. Always respect yourself and others will respect you right back."

Somehow, coming from her, nothing sounds phony.

CHAPTER 9

THE NEXT DAY WAS A VERY BAD ONE FOR JOEL AT SCHOOL. Someone, Kroeger probably, told the world about him seeing a shrink.

People were staring at him in the halls, and in science class someone whispered "schizo boy." He couldn't tell who it was. Joel's friends, like Michael Barron and VJ Madhani, said it was no big deal and tried to act casual, but that was awkward too.

And Wendy Shaeffer told him she couldn't go to the end-of-year dance with him. She didn't give any reason, she just said she couldn't go. It was all Mom and Dad's fault.

On Wednesday, Joel was afraid to go to school for the first time in his life. I didn't blame him. The high school is the kind of place where God help you if they think you're weak.

But Joel had no choice except to tough it out that one last day. He knew it and I knew it.

I was so mad at Mom for what she was putting Joel through, I didn't answer when she asked if I wanted a nectarine in my lunch. I just kept making my sandwiches and ignored the nectarines she put out on the counter. We didn't even say good-bye to her.

"I might have to fight Kroeger," Joel said, once we were out the door. "That's the only way people are gonna respect me again."

I shook my head. "No way. You get into another fight, Wagner'll bounce you. Anyway, that would be like admitting the whole thing got to you. Maybe just let it go, like it's nothin'. And if Kyle keeps at you, give him that look."

"You mean like this?" Joel stopped in the middle of the street. He made his left eye go a little smaller than the right one, curled his upper lip and flared his nostrils.

I burst out laughing. "You look like you just smelled someone's barf."

Then he tried to make the cold face again, but every time he tried, I made the smelling-barf face and he'd start laughing. By the time we got to school, my sides were hurting.

When I left Joel, he said, "Screw them, anyway. I don't care what they think."

Laura and I went around saying good-bye to the teachers we liked, which for me was just Mr. Morgan. I didn't want to hang around him too long, though, I had a kind of lonely feeling. Then I just more or less tagged along with Laura. She has a way of making people think they are her favorite person in the world when they're not. Especially males. Mr. Smith hugged her a little too long, I thought. Then we started running into a bunch of guys who asked Laura if they could dance with her at the dance and I got bored with that, so I wandered off. I found myself heading toward Mrs. Verdecchio's classroom, not because I wanted to see her but just to get my books and stuff. I was glad she wasn't there. I got my things and started to leave when the phone rang.

I'd never spoken on a classroom phone before, so I picked it up. It was Mr. Toth, the principal.

He sounded a little surprised to hear my voice.

"Is Mrs. Verdecchio there?"

"Not all there."

He hesitated a moment.

"Who is this?"

I don't know what got into me, but I said, "Robbie Burns." I rolled the "R"s.

Then I hung up. I knew Mr. Toth would come looking to see who it was, and I was in such a hurry to get out I almost ran over Mrs. Verdecchio, who came in the door just then. Her face lit up when she saw me.

"Roxanne! I'm so glad you –"

"Bye, Mrs. Verdecchio. Have a great summer." I was out of there.

Even though we'd been told to stay away, Laura and I went over to Silver Heights at noon. I wanted to make sure Joel was okay. We didn't want anyone to see us, so we walked all the way around the football field and behind the Nanking cherry bushes. Joel didn't really need us when we got there. Michael, VJ and Adam were eating with him. VJ told us Bruce Fisher had asked Wendy to the dance and she'd said yes. Joel's response to that was the very mature answer everyone uses when they're faking it.

He said, "So?"

Laura said Wendy was a pig, anyway.

Joel talked about what happened with the shrink, which I think was good, because then they knew it really was no big deal. Michael said the person that needs to see a doctor is Kyle, and Adam suggested that a bunch of people get together and jump on him. Adam always comes up with a violent solution to everything.

Anyway, Joel rejected that idea.

It was hot like anything out and I didn't feel like going back to school *at all*. Laura had to grab my hand, pull me up and drag me back over, and we were almost late for our big whoopie end-of-year dance. Which actually wasn't as boring as I expected. The DJ was fairly cool and I danced quite a few times with Gordie Burns, who got the Male Athlete of the Year Award.

Mr. Morgan asked me to dance and I was really embarrassed, but I did anyway. A group of grade-seven boys acted foolish and jumped around, no one was surprised by that.

At 4:30 P.M., June 27th, I left R.W. Douglas junior high school for the last time.

Joel didn't really want to go to his dance that night, but Michael and those guys persuaded him. Laura's mom had invited me to spend the night there, and said it would be all right for Joel and them to drop by after their dance.

Laura's backyard is basically the woods. While we were waiting for Joel and everyone to come, we built a fire in the pit and got some wieners out of the freezer and thawed them in the microwave. Then we broke some branches off the trees and whittled up some fancy little roasting sticks. Laura and I talked about stuff, like we always do.

We got onto the topic of guys, of course. I asked her if she still liked Brent Jackson and wished she hadn't broken up with him.

"No, he's a creep."

"Why?"

"Just is. He tried to stick his hand up my shirt. He's a loser."

"You mean like Kyle did to me?"

"No. Like for real, when we were kissing," she said.

"Why didn't you tell me about that?"

"I dunno. And then he went around telling his friends that we'd done it."

"Ew. Did he know how old you were?"

"No. I told him I was fifteen. But still."

"I never liked him. I mean, I told you. A guy you meet at the Stampede probably isn't the best investment you could make."

"That's what you say about every guy."

I shrugged. "You waste your time with a lot of losers.

You should be more selective, you could have anyone."

"Except Michael. He likes my best friend."

"Yeah, right."

I wanted to change the subject. I considered telling her about what Joel thought about Dad, but the time didn't seem right.

"Brent was cute, though."

"Yeah."

Anyway, we went on like that, just yakking, until Joel and Michael came at around 10:30, with VJ and Minnie Kazmaier, whose name is really Marion, but everyone calls her Minnie because of her squeaky voice. They left their dance early because the band was a bit too metal for them. Minnie told me that Wendy Shaeffer had seen them leaving and came running out and asked Joel where they were going. He froze her out, said "a party" and walked away. Couldn't have done better if I'd been there to coach him.

They said Bruce was drunker than any human being should ever be. I figured Wendy's parents must be crying that she was hanging out with Bruce instead of Joel. Old Brucie boy was on his way to Alcoholic World.

Laura brought her disc player out. We listened to some tunes and danced around and got crazy and ate hot dogs and chips until we felt sick. I worked up the nerve to ask Michael if he wanted me to make him a hot dog. He said yes, and I was so careful. It was the most beautiful-looking, perfectly roasted wiener ever. Michael said "Thanks, Rox," which he had never called me before. I spent the rest of the night wondering if it meant anything.

Laura's parents, as usual, were very cool about things, they never got excited about stuff like loud music late at night. Her mom came out about midnight and said we could swim. It would have been great, except I was the only one that had a suit along.

The guys left at 2:30, at which time Laura and I went to bed, but we kept talking until 3:00 or so. We didn't wake up until after lunchtime the next day.

Walking home, I was feeling about as good as I've felt in a year. The lilacs were still around, because of all the rain we'd had, and the smell of them reminded me of when I was young and didn't have any problems. Then I started thinking about my problems, and they didn't seem like much. I was thinking about how great it was going to be in high school next fall.

Then I got home. Mom and Dad called me into the den, to tell me Kyle Kroeger had been charged with assaulting an eleven-year-old girl at the community center. The police wanted to talk to me.

And that was June.

July

CHAPTER 10

At least I didn't have to go to the police station.

Two cops came to our house, a woman and a man, and the woman did most of the questioning. I guess that was so I wouldn't have to feel embarrassed. They asked me about what had happened at the high school that day, making me go over it so many times I thought I'd lose my mind. It was like, that incident was so small to me before, but describing it and reliving it seemed to make it bigger and bigger.

When I said it was really nothing much, the cop asked me, "Do you think it was okay for him to do that?"

Of course I said no. Then I asked, "What did he do to the other girl?"

"A group of kids were skating at the community rink. Kyle waited for this girl to be alone and pressed her against the brick wall. He forced her to kiss him."

"So like this was last winter?"

"Yes."

"Why is all this happening now?"

"The girl's parents have come forward. Maybe because they heard about what happened to you."

I started thinking Kyle was a really horrible person, not just a loser, which I've always thought. If I was eleven and that happened to me, I'd be scared. Then I remembered the pin prick at the swimming pool and what Matthew had said to me, which suddenly made sense. I knew I should tell the police and my parents about it, but I didn't. I didn't want to just then.

Instead I asked Mom and Dad, "Are you going to tell anyone else about this? You told Grandma, now you've told the police when I asked you not to."

Dad gave me a kind of warning, low-voiced "Roxanne," but Mom said, "No, we're not."

"Unless we deem it necessary, as your parents, to do so." Dad was sounding quite harsh, so I adjusted my attitude a little.

"Will I have to go to court?" I asked the police.

"Maybe. He'll be brought in for an assessment and we'll see from there."

I had to give a statement.

They sent me up to my room then, and I couldn't overhear what they were saying, and I was really tired, so I went to sleep.

Sometimes my parents seemed like a regular couple, worrying about their kids, calling family meetings and all that. Sometimes we seemed like normal kids with normal problems. Then I'd wake up and smell the nonreality. Number one, regular fathers don't cheat on their wives. Number two, regular parents don't send their perfectly sane child to psychologists. But then, number three, regular boys don't flip out swearing and beating people up. And number four. I'm not sure, but I don't think regular girls sit next to attic windows and stare out for hours and hours.

Anyway, putting aside the very irregular police visit start to the holidays, we got into a kind of regular holiday routine.

We started riding lessons out at Bragg Creek. We'd been taking lessons there every summer since we were eight and nine, we'd had the same instructor, Shirley, and I'd been on the same horse, Nifty, for four years. Joel got Gray again, but Shirley thought I was too advanced for Nifty, so she gave me Lightning. She was skittish and nervous. I told Shirley that, but she just laughed. "So am I," she said.

I felt very happy, in that way I always do when there's a stream nearby and flowers are there, being quiet and beautiful. It was very peaceful. I was glad Shirley was along to listen and respond to Joel's many millions of comments about birds, freeing me just to ride and think.

I was contemplating what it would be like to have my own horse one day. When I'm older, on my own, living outside the city on a ranch or acreage type of thing near a lake. I would have a horse and my husband would have a horse and every morning we'd get up early and ride together out to the lake. Then we'd go home and make breakfast and I'd take my second cup of tea up to the loft, where I would do my writing. Then, in the evening, we'd drive in our casual but expensive sports car to the city, where we'd meet Joel and his wife for dinner, after which we'd attend a literary event, where I would be honored for my work. My husband wouldn't be jealous or anything because he'd be successful at whatever he did. He'd be successful and respected. I was thinking what a good life it would be and how if we had kids, they'd never worry about anything. They'd just feel secure when they watched my husband laughing with me as we groomed the horses. My horse would be named Curtis, after Grandpa's horse.

I made supper when we got home. Spaghetti. Mom was chopping tomatoes for the salad and asked me about the riding.

"Great. I was making plans for my future and stuff."

"Oh!" She was delighted. "What sort of plans?"

"Just, career. Stuff like that."

I didn't want to tell her about the husband thing. She always thinks I spend too much time thinking about boys.

After riding lesson the next day, we went over to shoot some hoops at the community center. A bunch of people were there, but none that we knew well except Dawn and Matthew Cowling. I didn't exactly want to hang out with Matthew, so Joel and I went down to the court on the south side. Dawn followed us there. Although she was a bit boring sometimes, I felt sorry for her. Matthew was always twice as mean to her as he was to everyone else.

She asked me to walk over to the store with her. Joel didn't want to come and he wasn't interested in getting in on Matthew's game either. He went home.

On the way to the store, Dawn started talking really weird stuff. She told me that she used to have a crush on Joel and she told her mom about it and her mom said, "You can forget about that right now." When Dawn asked why, her mother said that her dad would freak if she ever came home with someone from a different race.

It kind of irritated me that she was bringing this up, so I said, "I don't think your parents have to worry about Joel asking you out anytime soon."

She said, "Well, my mom's not prejudice, just my dad."

That's how she said it, without the "d" on the end.

Then she asked, "Do you ever worry about that?"

"Worry about what?"

"About guys not being able to ask you out because their parents don't like people who are, you know, different?"

I said no. Because as if I wanted to talk to someone like her about something like that.

"My mom says she feels sorry for you and Joel growing up here, 'cause there aren't that many other, you know, kids around for you to go out with."

"Laura's dad is White. They don't seem to have a problem."

She shrugged. "Yeah, well maybe."

Then she finally got around to the whole point of her ramblings. "I've heard that Michael Barron's folks are prejudice."

I'd always suspected that she liked Michael, and it was obvious that she suspected the same of me.

It was quite a shock to hear that pathetic people like Mrs. Cowling feel sorry for *us*.

When I got home, I couldn't wait to ask Joel about Michael's parents.

"They nice?"

"Sure. Why?"

"Like, are they nice to you?"

"I said yeah, why?"

"Well, do you think they're bigots?"

He looked at me like I was crazy. "Nah, not at all. Who told you that?"

"Dawn."

"Why do you listen to her? You know she's nuts."

CHAPTER 11

EVERY DAY WAS STARTING TO FEEL EXACTLY THE SAME. We'd ride in the morning, swim and shoot baskets in the afternoon, come home for supper, play Scrabble or sit around talking in the evening, go to bed.

Until the night some of our friends decided to camp out down at the bridges. Dad said we couldn't go, so we asked about just visiting, not staying overnight. He said no to that too. It was so unfair, because even Laura's mom and dad said she could go. And I knew Michael would be there, and Dawn Cowling somehow got herself not really invited, but sort of tolerated along. I couldn't stand the thought of Michael being anywhere overnight with her. So, after Dad and Mom fell asleep, I talked Joel into sneaking out.

The sky was very clear. We could see the blackness of the river running along beside us, and the shimmering on the water made by the moon trying to squeeze light through the trees.

We went down the alley and then cut over toward Nose Hill and across the field to avoid being seen by our neighbors.

Total quiet except for some hooting. It wasn't really hooting, it was more like whirring. Joel said it was probably great horned owls, and who was I to argue with him about birds? Whatever. I felt strong, like it was my world and those were my owls.

We walked over the first bridge and under the second. Bruce said they'd be on the south side, and it took us only about five minutes to find them since they had a fire. Joel told them it was against the law. He sounded like such an old man. I was embarrassed.

Bruce said, "What would the cops be doing crawling over the bridges at, like, midnight, man? Relax."

Wendy Shaeffer was with him. She really liked Joel, before the entire school heard about him and the shrink. Still, because of that, Joel learned how shallow she was.

Laura, Dawn, VJ, Michael Barron and Adam Pichurski were there. And, of course, Bruce and Wendy. I was the youngest, as usual.

"I thought you guys couldn't come," Michael said to me, but before I could say anything my mouthpiece, Joel, spoke.

"We're not allowed to stay all night, but our old man said we could come for a while. We brought refreshments." He tossed our bag down on the grass. It was chips, cold-pack cheddar cheese, crackers and some grape juice in a Thermos.

Dawn took out the juice and tasted it. "Can we use this for mix?" She asked Bruce and he took a taste.

"Only if we want putrification, man. We'll use it as a chaser."

They had some beer and about a third of a bottle of whiskey. We used to pretend to drink rum when we played that lonely orphans game, but Joel and I had actually never tried any booze.

Adam tossed a bottle to Joel. I was afraid he was going to drink it, and I started regretting that I'd talked him into coming, but he didn't even open it. He just hung onto it. I knew he didn't want to drink it, but he was afraid they'd call him a wienie.

"Rox?" Adam held one up for me.

I sure didn't want to drink anything either, so I just gawked at him.

"She doesn't like it," Joel said.

"Can't you talk?" Adam asked me.

I just shrugged. Adam laughed and put the bottle down. Anyway, the only ones I could see that were actually drinking were Bruce and Dawn. Adam didn't even have any.

We just sat around like that. They had two tents, a little, ripped one that could fit three people if they really wanted to get close and a bigger one for four. I don't know where they thought everyone would have slept if Joel and I had planned to stay over. Adam dipped his crackers into the cheese without using the knife and people were telling him not to be a pig, and Dawn started laughing all the time because she was drunk, but we just ignored her. Wendy asked Joel if he wanted her to roast a marshmallow for him and he waited about fifteen seconds before he said "sure," but it was a sure like "It doesn't mean anything more than that, it's just a marshmallow."

Michael asked me if I wanted to walk down to the river with him to get some Coke out that was cooling. My heart started pounding. I said okay, but I had taken my shoes off and couldn't find them in the dark, and when I did find them, I saw Joel giving Michael the eagle eye. Then he had the nerve to say, "Don't be long," sounding just like Dad.

As we were walking, I tried to think of something funny to say to let him know that Joel was being, well, that it wasn't Joel's business to tell me not to be long. But before I could think of anything, Michael said, "If I had a sister, I'd probably act that way too. Especially if she looked like you."

All the blood in my body erupted into my head. I gulped so loud I think he may have heard me. What was he talking about? Looked like what? Unglamorously skinny and no breasts? I started to wonder if he was crazy or teasing me, but when I looked at him he was nice, just an incredibly good-looking guy that happened to be really nice. And then I don't know what got into me, but I started babbling about birds that can be found along the river, which is something I only knew about because of Joel, and I couldn't shut up. Thank goodness we found the Cokes or who knows what I might have started spouting? Then when Michael gave me two bottles to carry, his hand brushed my arm and I jumped back, and after that I could think of nothing to say. It was like my lips were glued shut and even when he asked me questions, I could only nod and it was dark, so he probably couldn't even see I was nodding. My hands were sweating and I dropped one of the bottles.

Joel was standing next to the fire waiting for us when we got back. He looked at Michael as though he had just robbed a bank or had spittle hanging from his chin or something.

"Take it easy, Joel, it was only a walk," Michael said.

"She's thirteen years old. Don't forget that."

I wanted to kill Joel. Michael might have thought I was fourteen.

"Where is everyone?" Michael asked.

"Dawn chucked in one of the tents and they're trying to clean it up."

Michael looked at me and raised one eyebrow.

That night for some reason everything seemed slow and dreamy and like I could stop my life right there, stay in that moment. I wished there was a way to hold onto the feeling, sitting around the fire with the toes of my right foot resting against Michael's leg.

Dawn was getting drunk because she thought somehow Michael would find that attractive, or think it was cool, or maybe want to get cozy with her or something. And I wasn't going to let go of what was happening between him and me, walk off and leave him with Dawn. Because I started believing that night that what Laura had been telling me was true. So I stayed until Dawn passed out.

We left a while after that, got in about three.

CHAPTER 12

UNCLE LEE AND SARAH CAME OVER THE NEXT DAY. I went out and hung around them for a while, smiling and everything, because if I didn't, I knew Uncle Lee would start shouting, "Where's my girl? Don't you like your old Uncle Lee anymore?" Or he might even start singing that song, "Roxanne," in a really high voice.

Dad tried to bring up something he saw on the news about rampaging Nazi types, but Uncle Lee changed the subject. He doesn't like to hear about that stuff. He says we shouldn't pay any attention to racists. He says they're not our problem.

Anyway, Wendy Shaeffer called Joel about an hour after Uncle Lee came and said she had something important to talk to him about, that she wanted to meet him at the first bridge. I wanted to go, but he said "You'd better stay here," like he was a fighter pilot going off to shoot aliens out of the sky. Like he was the CEO and I was the janitor.

There was nothing I could do except wait for him to get back, so I got a book and stretched out on the couch, pretending to read.

Mom and Dad were talking about how moody I'd been, and Uncle Lee and Sarah said I was supposed to be moody at my age.

"And Joel's worse than she is," Dad told them.

I was surprised they were talking about us at all, after what Dad and Uncle Lee had to say to each other the night I made dinner.

Then my mother started to say something about Joel as well, but she stopped when the door opened and Joel came in.

"Hey boy!" Uncle Lee shouted to him.

I hopped up from the couch, dying to know what Wendy had to say to Joel that was so urgent, and I could tell as soon as I saw him that something was up. Of course, we couldn't just go racing off to the attic without raising suspicion. We had to hang around casually, then drift off separately.

Wendy's news was that we were in for bad trouble.

After we had left the bridges the cops showed up. No one was sure how they knew we were down there, but we knew Matthew Cowling found out it was happening from Dawn and was mad about not being asked along. Mr. Cowling came at the same time as the cops and dragged her out of a tent and was shrieking and put her in the back of his car and drove off. So we were pretty sure it was Cowling. The rest of our friends were taken to the station and parents were called, and they were all charged with drinking while juvenile or acting like juveniles while drinking or something, and vandalism because of the fire. Wendy said none of them mentioned our names right then, but later Mr. Cowling beat Dawn up with a belt and Dawn got hysterical and said she was going to call the cops and press assault charges against him. He said, "You're not getting near a phone for a month, you slut," and she said our mother told their mother that hitting children with belts is abuse, and he said, "Were those Jacob kids there too?"

Dawn just kept crying.

But the point of the whole thing was to let us know a visit by the police to our house was coming.

CHAPTER 13

Joel and I spent the whole next day thinking they were going to show up any minute. We were jumpy and kind of hiding out in our attic and finally decided the best thing would be to tell Mom and Dad ourselves.

We expected them to yell and scream, not look at us and ask questions quietly. Their voices would go really high and tight at the end of a question, like, "Well, were you kids drinking down there?" and the pitch of "there" was at a level that would pierce a dog's eardrum. They said things like, "Didn't we tell you that you couldn't go?" and then they would ask something really obvious like, "So you just decided to go anyway?"

They said we lied to them. They didn't say, "you're liars," just "you lied to us."

I started to tell them it wasn't as bad as it sounded, but halfway through my excuses I realized, in fact, we had lied to them, so I shut up. What was the point? We all sat around not looking at each other and feeling really awful. They looked so betrayed.

The police came then, stayed for ten minutes. They didn't lay charges against us because we weren't at the bridges when they arrived and because everyone had said we weren't drinking and we hadn't helped set the fire. I think they just showed up to make sure our parents knew what we were up to. One of them was the lady cop who was here before about the Kyle thing. She was really nice to me, asked how I was doing.

After they left, Mom said she never thought she'd see the day that her own children would bring the police to her door, and how humiliating it was to have all the neighbors saying, "Oh, there are the police, paying a call to the Black people's house." I almost started to laugh then, because she was sounding so much like Uncle Lee. As if it's a billion times worse to have the cops come to your house if you're us than it is if you're anyone else. Then she said the weirdest thing to me, she said, "Were you kids fooling around?" meaning, "Were you kids having sex?"

I was so shocked, I said, "Don't be stupid," and immediately I was sorry, but Dad stood up then and his eyes were just wild and he shook his finger in my face and said, "Don't you ever speak that way to your mother, Roxanne!" Then he turned on Joel. "If you want to throw your life away, that's one thing, but I'm not going to stand by and watch you lead your sister down the same path. You're on shaky ground with me, Buster." So I burst into tears and screamed, "Why are you blaming him? He didn't force me to go. It was my idea." But Dad didn't believe me. He thought I was protecting Joel.

Dad said to get out of his sight. Just before he left the room, Joel whispered, in a really menacing voice, "No, you're on shaky ground." Dad whipped his head around and barked, "What?" But Joel just stared at him, with a very bad look in his eyes.

I tried to call Laura, but her mother wouldn't let her come to the phone. She was cold to me.

For a day and a half our parents said nothing more to us about what happened. Everyone was very polite to everyone else, but no one was really talking. Joel and I could hear them mumbling in low voices and we heard them on the phone, but we weren't able to make out what they were saying, except for when Mom said, "Do you think they're on drugs?"

Joel thought we should take off. Like always, he had a plan, but not a very well-thought-out one. Then again, I was always thinking, but I never had a plan.

He thought maybe we could go to Vancouver, we knew people there. I had about $135 saved up in the bank and $26 in my jar. Joel had the Canada Savings Bond that he got from Uncle Lee for winning the science fair last year. Plus he earned about $40 shoveling walks last winter. He said he wasn't sure if people our age were allowed to cash their own savings bonds, another example of how what you have is not really yours until you're eighteen.

I told him that wasn't even enough to get us to Kelowna, never mind Vancouver.

I was really irked to hear them talking about whether we used drugs or not, when we'd never even had a drink. I felt like running out to buy some drugs from Bruce, just to teach them a lesson.

Late the next night, Dad came to my room to see if I was awake, then went to get Joel. He told us we were going up to the farm to stay with Grandma and Grandpa for a while. He looked really, really sad. I asked him why it seemed like the whole world was falling apart just because Joel and I snuck out of the house one time.

"It's not you kids. It's not only you. Maybe we did overreact. Maybe some parents might think it was just a prank. But when you're out of this house, Mama and I have to know where you are and what you're doing. It's not a safe world out there. Do you understand that?"

Joel said, "You can't know where we are every minute forever. You can't know everything I say and do."

"No, not forever, son. But to think that we're lying up in bed sleeping while our two kids are out in the middle of the night ... in the middle of the night, at the railroad tracks and the river. And we don't even know it. What kind of parents do you think lie up in bed while their kids prowl the streets? Anything could have happened."

I said, "But nothing did happen, we weren't out taking drugs and jumping naked into the river, and if the cops hadn't been called, you never would have known about it and you wouldn't be feeling so bad right now. So why don't you just act like it didn't happen, if we promise not to sneak out again?"

He looked at me as though what I'd said didn't deserve an answer.

"Your mom and I have some things to work out as well and we think it would be good for you to spend some time at the farm. And your grandparents always want to see you, you know that."

"What do you mean you and Mom have things to work out? What's going on?"

"No, no, no. Nothing. We just need to sort through things."

I couldn't sleep that night. I crept past their bedroom and peeked in. Dad was sleeping with one leg out of the blankets. Mom was lying on her back.

And I thought Mommy, Mommy. Poor Mommy.

CHAPTER 14

ON TUESDAY, MICHAEL CALLED JOEL TO LET HIM KNOW a bunch of guys were going to play some basketball over at the outdoor courts behind the community center. Before they hung up, he asked, "Is Roxanne coming?"

I'd been thinking about him since the night down at the bridges, but in a way I was scared to see him again. My choice was between not seeing him for a long time and going along to the center, so I went.

Dawn was there. I told her I'd heard about her dad beating her up, and she said, "Yeah, my old man freaks out and grounds us for a year. Then he gets drunk and stays that way for a week and forgets about it."

I asked what her mom said and she said, "Nothin'."

I shrugged and said, "Parental love, eh?" She laughed her head off like that was the most hilarious thing ever.

We spent a little time talking about the cops and all that had happened to everyone. Bruce didn't take any of it too seriously, just laughed and said, "Now all the rest of you are criminals like me." No one had heard from Laura.

There were seven guys there and they needed one more to make the teams even. Bruce, joking, of course, because he believes girls only play basketball to give him a look at their bum and legs, asked if me or Dawn wanted to play. Joel said I was actually pretty good, so I ended up playing on a team with him and Michael and Larry Spencer, and the other guys were all shaken up because they believe that any boy basketball player is always going to be better than any girl and none of them had seen me play before.

The things I do best are dribbling and shooting from the corners, so I would bring down the ball and pass it to Joel or Larry, and they would get it to Michael under the basket because he's so tall. The other guys started doubling up on Michael to prevent him from getting the shot away, leaving me open in the corner. Michael would whip it to me and I'd score from there. Bruce's team was too proud to double up on me until I'd shot about six baskets. With two guys on me and two on Michael that left Joel and Larry completely open and Joel can hit from the top of the key every time. We wiped them. They were getting so ticked off, their elbows were swinging wild. When we were ahead 38 to 22, Michael said, "Oh, come on, it's just a game."

Later, when we were sitting around against the wall of the center drinking water, Larry started telling knock-knock jokes, the dumbest ones I'd ever heard. They didn't mean anything. Like, he'd say, "Knock, knock" and we'd say, "Who's there?" and he'd say, "Jim" and when we'd say, "Jim who?" he'd say, "Jim Pearson," which is the name of a guy at school. Then he'd kill himself laughing and the rest of us would look at each other. He did that about three times and every time we would refuse to say, "Who's there?" he would promise not to do it again, but then he would. Finally I said, "Knock, knock. Forty. Forty last time, shut up, idiot."

Then we all started telling the really poor knock-knock jokes that you always think are funny when you're about nine. We laughed and laughed. While I was lying on the grass laughing and the sun was baking me, while I was looking at Michael, everything seemed really okay, really good and just when I was wishing again that things could stay that way, Matthew and Kyle strolled up. We all stopped laughing.

Kyle looked right at me.

"You told the cops a buncha lies about me."

I stood up and started brushing the grass off my jeans. Everyone else stood up too, wondering what I was going to say. I couldn't think of anything intelligent, so something dumb came out.

"It's a free country."

Everyone burst out laughing.

Kyle pushed me. Joel, Michael and I all pushed him back. He fell down. Kyle looked at Matthew, but it was clear he wasn't feeling quite brave enough to step in. Kyle got up and started walking away. He didn't turn around, but we heard him say, "I'll get you, you bitch."

Joel started after him, but I called out sharply.

"Joel! Don't."

"We should," Bruce said. "We should get him."

I shook my head. "Don't. Just leave him."

Dawn looked really scared. "He carries a knife, you know."

Bruce laughed. "Anyone can get a knife."

I looked at Bruce, and started thinking about cutting him out of my social calendar.

"Let's just go home," is all I said.

Michael walked home with Joel, me and Larry. We talked about what losers the Kroegers and the Cowlings were.

Michael and I fell a few steps behind, so I got a chance to tell him I was going up to the farm for the rest of the summer. He didn't say anything. When we got to the corner where he turns off to his house, he put both of his hands on my shoulders and kissed me on the forehead and said, "See you at school next fall, I guess," and took off.

I didn't know what it was supposed to mean. The way he kissed me was exactly the way Uncle Lee would kiss me. But my shoulders where he touched me and my head where his lips were, felt like they were on fire.

I called Laura again when I got home and finally her mother let me speak to her. She whispered her answer when I asked what had happened to her after the bridges.

"They are *so* mad! They're acting like I joined a prostitution ring or something. They even said they might send me to a private school."

"Well, mine are sending me to the farm for the rest of the summer. They're totally freaking."

"The whole summer?"

"Yeah. What am I gonna do about Michael?"

"You mean Dawn and everything? I'll watch them for you."

Mom phoned the police again when we told her about what happened at the community center. The police said they would have to pay a visit to Kyle.

CHAPTER 15

WE LEFT THE NEXT MORNING.

On the drive up nobody talked. I was thinking about other trips we'd had when things were better, like the time we drove to Radium when I asked Mom and Dad what would be the very worst thing that Joel and I could do that would shame them so badly that they'd wish they were dead. Dad couldn't think of anything, but Mom didn't waste a minute. "Well, for Joel to stab an old homeless man and steal his meager belongings to buy drugs and for Roxanne to become pregnant by a pimp and have the baby but leave it wrapped in a dirty blanket in a garbage can in an alley." This caught us all a bit off guard and no one knew what to say, but all at once we burst out laughing and then we had to pull over to a rest stop we were laughing so hard. But there was no laughing, no talking this time.

When we got to the farm, Grandma said I could have the sunporch because Joel got it the last time we stayed there. He started to protest immediately, and I was stunned by her response. Normally, she would have said something like, "Don't you start that, Mister. We had a deal," but she didn't even give him a stern look. She sat on the bed and stared out the window.

"Okay. For now anyway. You start out in here and then we'll see." She looked at me. "That okay, Polka Dot?"

I was about to really throw a fit, because it was definitely my turn, but there was something in her face that stopped me.

Still, I was mad, so I frowned. "I guess so."

Joel was as surprised as me, I could tell he hadn't expected to get his way. When Grandma left to get more blankets, he looked at me and shrugged. "Sorry. I'll just stay in here tonight. Then I'll let you have it, 'kay?"

I got the bedroom across from Grandma and Grandpa's. Mom and Dad took the pullout in the basement.

Through the window from my bed, I could see Larson's Pond, the orchard, the hill between us and the Grebers' farm and about eight billion stars, even though the sky was still pink in the west. Orion was directly over my head.

When I woke up the next morning, Joel was already gone. Mom and Grandma were having coffee in the kitchen and Dad and Grandpa were out somewhere, so I grabbed a couple of apples and went looking.

I checked the barns first. When Curtis wasn't there, I knew that he and Joel had gone off somewhere together, and sure enough I found them in the pasture.

Curtis looked old, his back sagged and he walked pretty slow. Good old Curtis was the first horse we ever rode. Joel was brushing him and patting him and talking to him. I didn't have the heart to say, "Hey, Bud, I don't think he speaks English."

I plopped right down on my back in the grass. I grabbed Joel's binoculars and immediately spotted a bird way, way up.

"What's that?" I asked and without looking, Joel answered, "Osprey."

"You're not even looking!"

"Saw it earlier."

I knew if pretending to be interested in birds didn't get his attention, I'd have to be more direct, so I sighed really loud.

He finally looked at me.

"Maybe spending the whole summer here won't be that bad. We always spend time here in the summer anyway."

"Yeah, but it's like a punishment this time," I said.

Joel shrugged and went back to grooming.

"I won't see Michael."

"So."

"So, Dawn likes him."

"So, he likes you."

"Yeah, but I'm gone all summer. Maybe he'll forget about me."

"He doesn't like her type."

"What do you mean?"

"The drinking, smoking, staying-out-all-night type. The trashy type."

"The *trashy* type? You sound like her father."

"Shut up."

"Don't tell me to shut up. I'm trying to tell you something that I'm worried about and you're going on with some nonsense."

"Are you, like, in love or something?"

I started to cry.

Lately Joel had been trying to get me to stop crying all the time by saying, "You used to be tough," but that morning he just sighed.

"Oh, Rox, don't. I need you to stop that."

He got up and took Curt and went back toward the barns. I didn't feel like lying there crying by myself, so I followed him.

When we got near the house, we could hear loud voices, like people angry. We looked at each other, then both started running as fast as we could and burst in through the kitchen door.

Uncle Lee was standing close to Dad, who had his back turned to everyone. It was Uncle Lee's voice we'd heard, but as soon as we arrived everything got quiet. I had the feeling I was about to find out why Grandma had been acting strange, and I was right.

"Sit down," Dad told us. "We all need to talk."

And that's when everything started and stopped making sense all at the same time.

CHAPTER 16

"WHAT'S GOIN' ON?" I HAD TAKEN A CHAIR, BUT JOEL was still standing.

Everyone was looking at him.

"Son, we want you to know we love you very much. And we've never wanted to do anything that would hurt you ..."

Then Dad started to stumble over his words. He tried to start up again, then stopped. I could hear the breathing of everyone in the room, the heavy, heavy breathing of people whose secrets are being told. Mom had to take over. And this is what she said.

When she was growing up, she had a cousin named Mary Willis, who was the same age as her. She and Uncle Lee and Mary were very close and lived back and forth at each other's houses during the summers. A year or so after my parents met, Mary got engaged to a man named Lester Sherwood. My mom didn't like him, neither did Uncle Lee or my dad, but Mary and Lester got married anyway. They had a baby, then Lester went to jail for robbing a Brinks truck and Mary died. She had asked my mom and dad to be the godparents of her baby, so after she died, they ended up with a little boy – Joel. They got married two weeks after they adopted him.

And the reason they were telling us then was because Lester Sherwood had been out of jail for a while and wanted to get back into Joel's life. There was going to be a hearing and we were at the farm to be "sheltered" from it. And the reason Dad and Uncle Lee had been so hostile to each other for so many years was because Uncle Lee had always thought Joel and I should know the truth. And the reason Dad was sitting in his office with a blond woman named Cynthia was because she was their lawyer.

I had heard of people feeling like they were going to faint, read about it in books, but it had never happened to me before. I heard a great rushing sound, like wind in my ears and people's voices started to sound very far away.

"I have to go lie down," I said. I must have been shouting, because everyone looked startled. Joel went out the back door and I headed down the hall.

There was worry in Mom's voice when she said, "Kids," but Grandma said, "Let them go, Helen."

It's funny how you can be right about a lot of things, but wrong about them at the same time. We were right that Uncle Lee and Dad had problems that seemed bigger than they should have been. We were right that our parents' marriage was stressed somehow. We were right that there was something different about the way they related to Joel. But we were wrong about all the reasons.

The next few days were a blur. Mom and Dad had long talks with Joel and then went back to Calgary for some meetings with lawyers. Uncle Lee, Grandma and Grandpa talked a lot too, saying not to worry, that everything would be okay.

I tried reading *Flowers for Algernon* again. I started believing that when I read the final word, turned the last page, I would die, but I didn't. I realized stuff like that doesn't happen. Other stuff happens, but you don't die when you get to the end of a book.

I didn't have to try to numb my brain. It just was that way.

I didn't want to think or remember things. I didn't want to look back on memories like that stuff about my future life on an acreage with my husband.

I thought, someday I'll be fourteen, then I'll be eighteen, then thirty and then maybe I'll be a very happy person.

Joel had offered me the porch room and I'd said, "No, you have it." But I could see in his eyes that he thought I was pitying him, so I took the porch room, and I kept the woodstove burning every night.

And that was July.

August

CHAPTER 17

It seemed there was so much happening all at once, I couldn't find space in my head to try to sort it out. Since school ended there was the fight and Kyle Kroeger to think about, then Joel being sent to the doctor, then Michael, then my parents not getting along, then getting caught sneaking out of the house, having to leave Michael and go up to the farm. And I'd honestly thought all those things were problems. They weren't. Being told that Joel and I weren't really sister and brother was a problem.

It was so funny. Nothing had actually changed, only what we knew was different. But that knowledge made the sky look like a different sky, the grass was a different green; our grandparents were not our grandparents, they were mine. Joel started out trying to act as if everything was the same. But each day, he became more and more polite, less and less like Joel. Each day he moved a little farther away.

I tried to find things to talk about with him. I tried to make it a kind of us-against-them situation.

"They lied to us all along," I said one day when we were in the barn. Normally, Joel liked nothing better than for the two of us to sit around bagging about Mom and Dad. But he didn't say anything bad about them. He just nodded and kept brushing Curtis.

Then one day, we overheard Grandpa talking to the vet. Curtis had cancer and was going to be put down. I could see that he was sick. Flies would land on his eyes and he was too tired to blink or shake his head to get rid of them. His head hung. I knew inside myself that what Grandpa said was true, but Joel must have felt differently.

The next night he took Curtis and ran away.

The police came and interviewed me for a long time. They didn't believe that I didn't know where Joel went. Mom and Dad came back up to the farm.

At the end of the second day after Joel left, the police found Curtis, dead, near Flatbush. If Curtis hadn't died, they almost certainly would have caught up with Joel, how fast can an old horse with cancer move? But, on his own Joel moved fast. There was no sign of him anywhere.

Joel left a note for me near Curtis's body. It said,

Dear Roxanne,

Don't worry about me. I'm sorry Curtis died, I think from a heart attack. Tell Grandma and Grandpa I'll pay them back for the food I took. Please give one of these to Grandpa and keep one for yourself.

Love,
Joel

He had made two braids from Curtis's mane. The police took the note, but they let me keep the braided hair.

We stayed up at the farm for another week, everyone searching – the police, the neighbors, Mom and Dad. I wasn't allowed. I told them I thought Joel would go north, but they focused mostly west, because that's the direction they found Curtis. The police said runaways almost always headed for a big city, where they could get lost in the crowds, so they sent the information to Vancouver, Edmonton, Saskatoon, all the cities in the West.

Dad drove Mom and me back to Calgary after that, then he and Uncle Lee went back up to keep on searching. The police don't keep looking forever, especially for a runaway.

CHAPTER 18

My mother was out of her mind with fear and worry. Even having Grandma there didn't help. Mom wanted to be watching me all the time, but I could tell she really wasn't able to think about me.

If I got a phone call, she'd stand there listening. If I said I was going out for a walk, Mom would say, "Gee, I could use some air, I'll go with you." But then she'd get her coat and sit on the couch, staring at the wall. And I didn't have the heart to leave her there, so I wouldn't bother going.

Day after day with a knot in my stomach and nothing to be done about it.

I was thinking a lot about God. Grandma was always saying things happen as part of a plan. So I was thinking, if that was true, then God must have somehow planned for Curtis to get cancer right after our parents decided to tell us about Joel, and all of that would be piled on top of everything else and make Joel crack under the weight. It seemed like a very bad plan. I asked Grandma what she thought of God's plan and she said she'd let me know later.

"When later?"

"Later. When Joel's married and has kids of his own who are acting up and we're all sitting around laughing about the time he ran away."

I've never, ever thought my grandmother was lying to me, except for that moment, when she said one day we would laugh.

Then one morning, it was a Thursday, Mr. Morgan came over. It was very odd, seeing him at my house, looking like a person and not a teacher. He had read in the paper about Joel being missing and tried to call, but Grandma had answered the phone, didn't know who he was and forgot to pass the message on. So he just came. He was the first person who was calm about the whole thing. Not calm like, "I don't care," but calm like, "Everything will be okay."

He shook my mom's hand and she said, "Good of you to come by, Dave. We appreciate the interest you've shown in our kids over there at Douglas." I hadn't known his name was Dave.

Maybe it was just having someone there who was a kind of outsider, or having to make tea, or not wanting to be weak in front of him or whatever, but it was very good for all of us. It was a distraction.

I was sitting out on the deck when he left. He sat down beside me and asked if I was okay. He also said, "Joel's smart. He'll be fine." It was a comfort.

I thought if I wasn't already out of my mind in love with Michael, I'd go for Mr. Morgan.

After he left, I listened to music for the first time in weeks. It was heartbreaking, like music is. Too beautiful and sad and reaching down too far into parts of me that no one knows.

Dad and Uncle Lee came back that night. They had driven hundreds of kilometers, east, west and north of Athabasca, with no sign of Joel. The police told them they would do better to go home, that Joel was more likely to be in Calgary, hiding out with a friend, than anywhere else. I had already thought of that, that maybe he'd been in touch with Michael or VJ. But Mom called their mothers. They didn't know anything.

Life became a totally abnormal, surreal sort of thing. Dad got up and went to work, Mom fussed over the tomato plants in the garden, Grandma was there, Uncle Lee and Sarah were over a lot. Sarah and I were making dinners and begging everyone to eat them. We talked about recipes.

Somehow, we all started sleeping in the den, on pullouts, on mats, in sleeping bags. It was like we needed to feel safe, all in one room.

Laura came for a sleepover on a Friday. I was happy to see her at first, but then she started getting on my nerves. She was probably trying to take my mind off Joel by talking about other things. People and what they were doing, gossip and stuff. She told me Kyle Kroeger had been sent to a group home temporarily. I didn't care.

I asked if she'd seen Michael, and her face got a strange look. Defensive.

She shrugged. "Yeah."

"Has he been hanging out with Dawn?"

"No. I don't think so. Hasn't he called you?"

"No. Have you seen him?"

"I saw him at the show, the pool a couple of times."

"Was he with anyone?"

She didn't answer, and then I knew. I just knew.

"With you?"

"We're friends. We were just getting together."

I didn't let her finish. I didn't ever want to see her again.

"Get out."

"Rox."

"I said get out!" I was screaming.

My mother came bounding up the stairs to find out what was going on. Laura started to cry and ran past her.

"Roxanne, what is it?"

"Get her out!" I put the pillow over my head. I assume my mother left the room, because she wasn't there when I opened my eyes. I assume Laura's father came to pick her up. I assume the others slept in the den that night. I lay on top of my covers with all my clothes on, thinking about Joel and wondering where he was and if he was alive.

CHAPTER 19

THE NEXT MORNING I TOLD MY PARENTS I WAS GOING TO ride my bike to Laura's house.

"Well I should think so," my mother said. "You owe her an apology. I don't know what went on between the two of you, but she was very upset when she left here."

I nodded.

I got Laura's blue sweatshirt, which I'd been borrowing for about two months, because she said it looked better on me anyway. I got the silver bracelet she gave me for my twelfth birthday and the teddy bear Brent won for her at the Stampede, but that she didn't want. I put them all in my backpack, got on my bike and rode through the ravine and down along the river. When I got to her house, her mother was in the yard, weeding the butterfly garden.

"Hi," I called out to her.

"Roxanne!" She was surprised to see me. She wiped her hands on her jeans and stared at me, like, what do you want? I didn't say anything. I guess she didn't know what to say either. Normally, she just would have told me to go in.

Finally she said Laura was in her room.

I'd been in Laura's room so many times, it was almost like my own. It was strange, looking around at all her stuff, walking on the hardwood floor, knowing it was the last time I would do that. She was lying on her bed with her hands behind her head. The only part of her that moved when I walked in was her eyes. I must have had an awful expression on my face, because her eyes looked scared. All the way there, I had been thinking of terrible things to say to her, to hurt her like she had hurt me. But when the time came to say them, I was afraid I would start crying. I opened my backpack, dumped her stuff on the floor, turned around and walked out. Without saying a thing.

Her mom watched me hop on my bike. I waved to her and rode home.

She must have called my mother after I left, because when I got there, Mom was waiting for me on the deck.

"Roxanne," she said, but I walked right past her into the house.

"You're worried about Joel. Don't take that out on Laura. You need your friends."

"I don't have any friends." I headed up the stairs to the attic. I curled up on the cushions and went to sleep and slept all the rest of that day and all night, until the next morning.

I could hear my mother and father having breakfast together when I went downstairs. Not talking, just moving plates, pouring tea, clearing throats. I wanted so badly to hear them talking to each other, the way they did before, when Joel and I were little and used to listen in on them as they folded laundry together, or ate breakfast or all the things they used to do. I sat on the steps and listened to them not talking to each other. Then it occurred to me it was ten o'clock and Dad should have been at work.

I went into the kitchen, got out a bowl and some cereal and sat down at the table with them.

My mother reached out her hand and placed it on my forehead, checking to see if I had a fever. Without thinking about it, I brushed her hand away. Dad pushed his chair back, but didn't stand up. There was a moment or two of silence before he spoke.

"We want to talk to you."

I nodded, then went back to my cereal.

"Do you have any idea where Joel is?"

"No."

"Did he tell you anything before he left? Anything about us?"

My mother's face was trembling.

"He told me lots of stuff about you."

Dad put his hands over his face and started to cry. It was the first time in my life I'd ever seen him do that. I was so amazed, so stunned. I looked at my mother, who wasn't looking at me at all. She kept her eyes on Dad, then reached out and touched his shoulder.

He wiped his eyes, then managed to tell me what he wanted to tell me.

"It's my fault," he said. "I blame myself. Lee was right. I should have told him, but I didn't want him to know about Lester. Sittin' up in jail all these years, he's crazy. He was crazy before he went in. I didn't want Joel burdened with all that."

What did he want to hear from me?

He tried to collect himself. "Roxanne, if you know where he is, you have to tell us. Has he gone to find Lester? Did he say anything to you about that?"

"No! I told you, I don't know where he is. If he's gone looking for that Lester guy, I don't know anything about it."

I felt a surge of anger toward them.

"Don't you believe anyone? You say it's your fault Joel ran away, then you keep asking me and asking me. I told you, I don't know where he is!"

I left the house.

I didn't know what to do. I had no one to talk to.

I went to the swimming pool, where I saw all the people who used to be my friends. I stood outside the chain-link fence and watched them. Laura was there, Michael, VJ, Dawn – they were all diving for the puck in the deep end of the pool. I wished I was one of them and not me. I wished I was Laura, beautiful and so sure everyone liked her, and so able to go on living and having fun even though her best friend wasn't her best friend anymore.

I almost went in. I pictured myself going into the changing room and getting my bathing suit on and walking out on the pool deck and having someone notice me. I imagined someone, Michael maybe, inviting me to join them.

But then Dawn saw me. She started treading water, just staring at me as she scooped her hands back and forth under the surface of the pool. The others turned to see what she was looking at. I walked away as fast as I could, forcing myself not to run. I thought I heard Michael calling my name.

I took the bus to the mall and went to a movie.

CHAPTER 20

My grandmother tried to make me understand why everything had happened, that my parents loved Joel and me the same as they always had, that Uncle Lee loved us too. I didn't really want to hear about them or their problems or how they needed me to stop being angry with them.

Grandma didn't want to leave us, I could tell. But Grandpa needed help with the cows, so she went home to the farm the next day. My parents and I were left to ourselves.

It was very funny being around them then. Like we were all strangers, just some people who had been staying together. Like they looked at me as a person, not as a child. Like they accepted whatever I was feeling and weren't going to force me to be friends. I felt free. I felt very alone.

The next day I rode my bike around the neighborhood. I bumped into Minnie Kazmaier, who was just back from vacation and didn't even mention Joel or anything that was happening to me. I realized she hadn't heard. It was refreshing. She said there was going to be a party at the house of someone I didn't know. I had nothing else to do and nowhere else to go, and another night alone with my dark thoughts wasn't too appealing. Maybe I also thought Michael would be there, and even though I was pretty angry with him by then, I couldn't help it, I wanted to see him. I told my parents I was going to an exhibition basketball game at the university. Dad offered to give me a ride, which I accepted. After he dropped me off at the university gym I called a taxi.

I knew as soon as I got to the party, I was in way, way over my head. It was out in the southwest somewhere, in some district I've never heard of, at a condominium rented by some eighteen-year-old who was covered in Satanic-looking tattoos. The whole place smelled of urine and spilled booze, except for the basement, which smelled like grass.

The only people I knew there were Minnie and a girl named Lisa Heddle, who I'd never liked very much. Guys were hitting on them hard, very unpleasant guys that looked sort of like those people you see on the news rioting after hockey games. I think for the first time in my life I was glad to be the younger, not-as-good-looking, ignored friend.

Then both Lisa and Minnie disappeared into what I presume was a bedroom with a couple of the guys and I was left alone. I wanted to go home. Uncle Lee once told me if I was out with people who were drinking I should call him, no matter where or when, but I couldn't call Uncle Lee, so I thought I'd call a cab. I wandered around the house until I found a phone but someone was on it. I waited until the guy gave me a bad look, then drifted back into the living room.

I sat by myself on the ratty old couch for a long time. I was thinking about transcendental meditation and wishing I knew how to do it. I tried to put myself in a trance. Whenever anyone looked at me I could tell they were thinking, "What's she doing here?" So I didn't make eye contact, I went a whole hour without speaking, which is strange when you're in a really crowded room. But even though I was trying to appear invisible, to look like an empty shell, just a body whose soul had gone off elsewhere, someone found his way to a spot on the couch beside me. His feet smelled. I could actually smell them. He leaned over to me and said, "Are you Filipino?" I wondered if it was a trick question. Like what if Filipinos weren't allowed at that party and he was in charge of keeping them out? Or what if Blacks weren't allowed and he was trying to trick me into identifying myself. I decided to go with the truth.

"No."

He was so drunk or something his words came out slurry.

"Well, what are you?"

I closed my eyes, but he was still there when I opened them.

"Canadian," I said.

"Oh. From Jamaica?"

"No."

"Oh. 'Cause I heard Filipino chicks are great in bed."

He smiled at me and I saw several very rotten teeth. I said the only thing I could think of to say.

"Is that right?"

Just then a less scary-looking guy came along carrying three bottles of beer. I vaguely recognized him from Joel's school, so I jumped up, as though I'd been waiting for him. I snatched one of the beers from his hand.

"Thanks!" I shouted, and followed him down the hall. When I was sure Mr. Rotten Teeth and Smelly Feet couldn't see me anymore, I gave the bottle back.

"You can have it." He smiled at me and he had a nice smile.

"I just wanted to get away from that ... person," I said.

The music was quite loud, so he leaned in closer to me. "Good thinking."

He took the beer out of my hand, twisted off the cap and gave it back to me. I had a sip. It was awful.

"You're Joel Jacob's sister, right?"

I nodded.

"Heard he split."

I nodded again, then took another sip of the beer.

"You wanna go outside?"

Third time, I nodded again. We wound our way through all the people and out a back door. There was one of those cushiony backyard swings, which we sat down on.

His name was Stewart Duncan. He was going into grade twelve. We talked about the high school and the basketball team and about Joel being a good athlete. Every time I finished a bottle, he gave me another one. Then he kissed me and gave me a cigarette. My brain was getting fuzzy, but I remember thinking Joel would disapprove of me smoking. I had never had even one puff of a cigarette before. I choked and coughed and started to feel very sick. Stewart said he was going to get me a glass of water.

By the time he found me again, I was throwing up on the hollyhocks. I thought I was going to die, and there were all these strangers around me, none of whom wanted to touch me or help me and who could blame them? Then I heard a familiar voice. It told someone to find my jacket and shoes, and to get me into the back seat of a car. I looked up. It was Laura. I didn't know how she got there. I didn't know whose car it was. I didn't care. Laura got in beside me. She told whoever it was to drive to her place, and all the way back across the city she watched me. Whenever I needed to throw up, she told him so he could pull over. We had to do that three times.

We got to Laura's house eventually. She told Mr. Whoever to take me around to the back door. She went in the front way and must have faked her parents out somehow, because when she came to the back door and took me upstairs we didn't run into them. She put me in her bed, took off my socks and shoes. The last thing I remember is hearing her call my mom to tell her I was spending the night there.

CHAPTER 21

IN THE MORNING WHEN I WOKE UP, LAURA WAS WRAPPED in a sleeping bag on the floor. I sat on the edge of her bed and watched the movement of her breathing. She looked peaceful. I wanted to talk to her so much. She had always been the person I told everything to, even things I never told Joel, because he's a boy and you can't tell a boy everything.

But I couldn't see a way to go back to our old friendship.

I wrote a little note saying "thanks for helping me out," stuck it to the dresser, slipped down the stairs and out the door, and walked home.

Around about then I knew I really needed to think about what to do. Because I couldn't just go on like that, could I? I was falling to bits. I couldn't go on throwing up in front of strangers and doing things I really didn't want to do just because I felt so awful. None of that was bringing Joel back. None of that was making me stop loving Michael in such a terrible, hurting way.

The only thing was, I didn't know what to do about any of it. I really didn't.

Then, later that night I heard tapping on my window. I was dreaming about riding the Tidal Wave at the Stampede, but then it turned into a tree I was climbing and the tapping was a woodpecker. Even after I woke up and realized the tapping was real, I still thought it was woodpeckers for a minute. So I lay there really confused, wondering, why are woodpeckers tapping at my window?

I got up to look, finally, and saw Michael in my backyard. He gestured for me to come down, so I did. I put on my jeans and my housecoat and went downstairs and out the back door.

Over his shoulder he had a very flexible twelve-foot tent pole. That's what he'd used to wake me up.

He had come to tell me Joel was waiting at a phone booth in Calling Lake. I was still sleepy and a little stunned that he was there. I said, "But I don't know the number," and he laughed and said, "It's okay, Roxanne, I've got it."

We headed for the booth over at the community center, trying not to look like two teenagers out in the middle of the night making a drug deal.

As we walked, I threw a million questions at Michael – "Is he all right?" and "Where is he?" and all that, and "When did he call, how did he get through without your parents knowing?"

Michael didn't know very much, except that Joel

had called his house twice, hung up when Michael's mom answered, and finally got Michael on the third try. He stayed on the line only long enough to give Michael the number and tell him to go get me really late, after people were asleep.

It was cold, one of those nights when you know very well it's summer but it won't be for much longer. I could see our breath as we talked. Michael gave me his jacket when he saw me shivering, then I had to watch him shiver. I must have looked very attractive, dressed in my slippers, jeans, pajamas, housecoat and Michael's bomber jacket. With my braid half in and half out.

Michael had brought a whole bunch of change along; he thought of that on his own, because of course it was a long-distance call. My hands were shaking. Joel answered after four rings.

The first thing I said to Joel was, "It's me," and he said, "Who did you think I would think it was?" And I laughed.

"What took you so long to answer?" I asked.

"I was asleep. I've got the tent pitched a little way from here in the bushes and I fell asleep waiting for you."

"Are you all right?"

"Sort of. Did you get that braid from Curtis?"

"Yeah."

"Is Grandpa really mad at me for killing him?"

"You didn't kill him. He was going to die anyway."

He didn't say anything for a minute, and when he finally did, his voice was really quiet. "Curtis caught a bad chill. It rained for a couple of days, hard, and there was nothing I could do to keep him warm or dry. He sat down and wouldn't get up again no matter what I did, and then he died."

"I've been really worried, Joel. Everyone down here has been going crazy. I've even wondered if you were dead."

Silence.

"Are you coming home?"

"No."

"Come home."

"The reason I'm calling is, I need some money."

I waited for him to go on.

"I met a guy who says he has a plane. He'll fly me into the Northwest Territories for two hundred bucks and he says I might be able to work on his crew up there."

"What does his crew do?"

"I don't know."

"Have you seen his plane?"

"No."

"Do you think an adult who says he's willing to fly a fourteen-year-old to the Northwest Territories is the best person to hook up with?"

"I told him I'm sixteen and I live with foster parents that don't want me anyway."

"That's not true. It's a bad plan. You have to come home."

"I actually need about three hundred. To pay him and get settled up there."

"Where am I supposed to get three hundred dollars?"

"Cash in my bond. And lend me some of yours."

"I can't cash your bond without Mom and Dad knowing."

"Can you get some money from them? Tell them you need it for something?"

"What am I going to tell them that won't make them suspicious? I'm not going to steal from them."

Another long silence, then, "I didn't really expect you to help me. I just wanted to let you know not to worry. I'm okay."

"Joel, please come home."

"No."

"Can I tell Mom and Dad you called?"

There was a long pause.

"I don't want you to. But you'll do it anyway."

I could hear it in his voice – you'll tell them, because you're their child and I am not. You and they are family. I am not.

And I couldn't bear it. "I'll get you the money. If you'll let me bring it to you. I want to see you."

"I don't think so."

"How far are you from Athabasca? I'll take the bus and meet you there."

He was quiet for so long I thought maybe he had hung up. I started to panic.

Finally, he said, "Okay. I'll meet you at the Athabasca bus station on Tuesday night. I'd like to see you too."

I said good, and hung up, and Michael and I stood there, shivering.

Back at home we drifted out at the side of the house for a while, at first talking about Joel and what he'd said and what I should do. Michael offered to help me get the money. Then he asked, "What about Laura?"

I wasn't sure what he was asking, what about Laura helping, or what about Laura and me and everything that happened. I got quiet and then he got uncomfortable, and then I said I had to go in.

"Oh ... So do you want me to help about the money?"

"I'll call you, okay? If I need anything."

Michael shrugged. " 'Kay."

I gave him his jacket back and watched him walk off down the street.

CHAPTER 22

THE WHOLE THING ABOUT RAISING THE MONEY AND making a plan was complicated, as I expected. When I said I wanted to go up to the farm, Dad was so pleased that I was showing an interest in doing something that he agreed right away. But Mom didn't like the idea. She listed a bunch of reasons why I shouldn't, none of them being the truth, which was that she was afraid to let me out of her sight.

They argued back and forth for a half hour, while I tried to figure out what I should do to convince her. When she said maybe they should have kept a closer watch on Joel and that might have prevented the whole thing from happening, I saw my chance.

"I don't think so, Mom. I think the opposite."

"What are you talking about?"

"I think, you know, you were watching him all the time. He felt like you didn't trust him."

That worked, and there was lots more discussion, but the next day they phoned Gram and Gramp to let them know I was coming, gave me some money and put me on a bus.

I needed extra time beyond when I was expected to arrive, so I got off at the Red Deer stop and called to tell Grandma I would be arriving a day later. She said sure, then asked to speak to my mom. I said she was in the shower. I hung up, feeling scared and stupid and like the whole thing wouldn't work out, but there was nothing I could do about the dumbness of the plan.

I slept most of the way to Edmonton and would have slept between Edmonton and Athabasca too, except an old man got on and wanted to talk to me. He wanted to know where I was going. I was so tired of lying. So I told partial truths. I said my grandparents had a farm in the Athabasca area. I said my brother had been "up there" for the summer. He was a nice old man, completely bald and with an enormous nose. He wore small, round glasses with gold frames. Very cool. He was on his way to see his granddaughter's new baby in some little town I'd never heard of. He gave me a bag of honey-roasted peanuts.

After he got off the bus, I had time to think about things. If I could only bring Joel home, everything else would work out. That's what I was thinking as I fell asleep, feeling calm and ready.

CHAPTER 23

JOEL WAS WAITING FOR ME WHEN I GOT OFF THE BUS. HE looked older. His clothes were dirty and he had a hat pulled down low to cover his face. He looked like someone Mark Twain might have dreamed up.

He didn't smile, or say he was happy to see me or anything. He just said hi.

We walked about twenty minutes into the bush, where he had a camp, a very well-camouflaged one. I didn't see it until I bumped into the tent.

He lit a small fire and gave me some tea made from spruce needles, which tasted bitter, until he added some honey that he'd got from who-knows-where.

"So, tell me everything," he said.

He had questions about the search for him and what the police had to say and all that sort of thing. He was surprised to learn they actually weren't looking for him anymore.

"Like, they're keeping an eye open, but they're not sending all available men out on a ground search every day."

For the first time, he grinned. "Yeah, guess it's not like I'm the most important person in the world."

I answered his questions carefully, thinking all the while about my resolution not to lie anymore.

I wanted to hear about everywhere he'd been and what he'd done and how he'd survived. But first I told him I thought it was time for him to come home. I told the truth about why I'd come, which was to try to talk him into it. I said I wasn't going to lie to Mom and Dad anymore. I thought he might feel differently about telling me stuff if he knew that first, and I was right.

"So you're on their side?"

"Why does there have to be a side? I just think this running away is a bad idea and you should come home. I feel like I'm on your side, but if you think I'm not, that's up to you."

The fire was dying a little. Joel took a stick and stirred it around and made it lively.

"There's a trial thing, or something. Some kind of court case with that Lester."

"He's my father. That Lester."

I didn't know what to say.

"Maybe I should go stay with him."

He wasn't saying it to be pouty or as a threat or anything. He was honestly saying it.

"What would I do then?" I asked. Like what would I do without my brother? I wasn't saying it to be selfish. I was just wondering. "You know how Mom and Dad are."

He nodded. That had always been the thing with Joel

and me. We knew what the other one meant, without saying too much.

I went on. "I think they can't help it. They're really trying to do their best. They really love you. I can tell by the way they've been since you left."

He had his arms wrapped around his knees and his head down, he was rocking back and forth. I knew he was thinking thoughts I could never understand, because who knows what it's like to find out your father and mother aren't your parents, your sister isn't your sister, unless it's happened to you? So I just sat.

We talked for a long time more, about people we knew and school and things we had done when we were younger. Joel told me he had called Dr. Leavens three times since he'd run away, but he asked me not to tell. Because Dr. Leavens would get in trouble if people found out she'd heard from him and hadn't told. We talked for a long time without stopping because we knew each other that well. Then we crawled in the tent and went to sleep.

The next morning, I helped Joel pack up his tent and gather up all his things. When we get back to the bus station, the police were there looking for us. Dad had called Grandma and Grandpa and learned about my phone call and they knew I'd tricked everyone and that I must have been on my way to meet Joel. They traced my bus ride and called the Athabasca RCMP and that's how they caught up to us. But it didn't matter anymore. Joel was coming home with me.

CHAPTER 24

When we got back to Calgary, the police came over to interview all of us, in order to close the missing-person file. They asked Joel why he ran away and he said, "I can't remember." They asked him if there was violence in our home, or any other type of abuse, and he said no. They asked if he was planning to run away again and he said no. They left and he went back up to the attic.

Grandma had arrived by then. When the police were gone, she came out and sat on the back deck with me. She asked what I was thinking about.

I was thinking how my mother was going to look back on the summer of all the police visits.

The summer that was not like any other summer.

"I don't know from one day to the next what's going to happen. You know, Gram?"

"Oh, honey, I do know. I know. It's a hard time of life. It's a dangerous time. You've got to hold on, though, Roxanne. You're the youngest in your little family, but in a funny way, everyone depends on you. You're like my mother, she had strength like you have, the kind of strength that people anchor onto. Use that strength to get through all this. And don't be afraid to pray."

"That doesn't help me."

"Well, maybe not, not right now. But it helps your grandma and she's going to keep on."

"Where do your words go, when you pray? Who are you talking to?"

"You're asking me how I know, and I don't have the answer. I don't know how to prove to you that prayer has meaning. I only know I believe it does."

We were quiet together for a few minutes.

"What are we going to do? What will we do now about Joel and how he feels and everything?"

"Just let it heal like everything always does. One thing you've got to do is stay busy. You're a smart girl, and smart people just have to look around this world and see that things aren't so good. That's frightening to anybody, not just a kid trying to sort out her life. Keep busy, keep active. Thinking too much is depressing. When you feel down, don't go sit up in that fort of yours. Get out and go bowling with your friends."

"We don't go bowling."

"Then do whatever it is you do. Just don't do anything silly."

"You sound like Mom. You mean like don't have sex, right?"

She laughed. "Yes. That's what I mean."

"Has Mom talked to you about Michael?"

"Yes."

"Well?"

"He sounds like a nice boy. I trust your judgment. You're a little young, I agree with your mother there, but I think maybe she's forgotten about Floyd Henderson. He gave her an engagement ring when she was fourteen." Grandma shook her head. "He'd been saving for a car, but took the money and spent it on this cheap little ring. I had to make her give it back to him, phone his mother. Helen cried for days. Then she got interested in Willie Haynes. Forgot all about poor Floyd."

She was holding my hand between her very soft ones, and she looked at me for a long time. "But you be careful, Polka Dot. Don't let anyone hurt that little heart of yours."

"Oh, there's nothing anyway, Grandma. We're just friends now."

"That's all right too. Friends count for something."

CHAPTER 25

TWO STRANGE THINGS HAPPENED AT THE FAMILY COURT. I mean, the whole thing was really strange, with us being there and Dr. Leavens giving testimony about Joel. It came out that Lester had this stupid idea that Joel had been left some money, and Lester figured he might be able to get some of it. There wasn't any, of course, and Joel said he didn't want to have any contact with Lester. But the one strange thing was realizing Joel looked a bit like Lester, but he was more like our dad. Like the way they both stand with their hands hanging the wrong way. I guess that's something Joel learned, not something he was born with.

The other strange thing was that Kyle Kroeger was there. He was supposed to have a meeting of some kind, but his parents didn't show. He was with two grim-looking adults, I assumed from that group home he was sent to.

Things were quiet around the house the next day. Joel was up in the attic, my parents and Grandma were doing a lot of heavy talking. I set out to go for a walk, not really intending to go anywhere in particular. I just sort of headed west along the bike path. I had my head down, so I didn't see Matthew Cowling riding toward me. He squealed on his brakes and swerved right two inches in front of my feet.

"Heard your loser brother took off. Didn't think he had the jam."

I gave him a look, then walked around his bike and continued on. He followed me, at first walking his bike, then he dropped it so he could jog around in front of me, in my way. I was thinking, what should I do, considering that he had pricked me with a pin in the swimming pool. You never know what guys like him will do. I stopped walking. We stood looking at each other. I started thinking maybe I could take him in a fight – he's not very big, and, yeah, neither am I, but I'm strong. But then I thought, do I really want to get in a fistfight on the bike path? What if one of my mother's friends drives by? And then I thought, do I really want to go through this with Matthew Cowling every time I see him?

So, I said, "He's back." In just a normal voice, like he was a regular person who had asked about Joel and I was just answering his question.

He sneered. He had a big, fat, white pimple on his lip, about to burst. "What?"

"He's back. He went up north for a while, but he came back."

It dawned on him that I was either unaware that he was trying to scare me, or maybe it dawned on him that I was pretending, but anyway, the expression on his face changed. It went from that slit-eyed look stupid people get when they're trying to figure out what's going on, to a casual kind of "somebody is having a conversation with me" look.

"Oh yeah?"

"Yeah, he got all the way up to Calling Lake. Saw some animals and stuff. Lotta birds."

"Cool."

"Anyway, I gotta get going."

"You goin' down to Laura's?"

"Yes," I said.

"Cool. 'Kay, see ya, eh?"

"Yeah. See ya, Matthew. See ya at school."

He jumped on his bike and rode away looking quite happy. I wondered if he knew about Kyle.

I kept walking, down the path past the saskatoon bushes. I tasted a berry, but they were still bitter and hard. The wet spring, I think. Plus, it was late for saskatoons anyway. My feet walked me along, and my brain was so busy thinking about people like Kyle Kroeger and Matthew Cowling and how they're different from people like me and Joel. They're on a different path. They're going to have different lives than us. Kyle was already started on his different kind of life, in the group home. I'd heard he wasn't coming back to our school, and for all I knew I'd never see him again. And Matthew, he'd be following Kyle soon enough. I was thinking about all that, how I probably wouldn't have to worry about them bothering me again, because Kyle was gone and my little trick with Matthew had worked. And how if they did bother me again, next time I would just tell the cops. I was so totally wrapped up in my walking and thinking that I didn't even notice I actually was on my way to Laura's.

There was no answer when I rang the bell, but it didn't look like no one was there – the curtains were open for one thing. I went around to the backyard and, sure enough, Laura was swimming in the pool.

"Hi." I sat at the edge of the pool on crossed legs.

"Hi," she said, but she kept swimming. I didn't really blame her.

"Joel's home."

"I know. Your mom phoned my mom yesterday."

It wasn't even a sunny day, there were clouds and I was wishing I had a jacket. Still, the water looked pretty good. They always kept it warm. I dipped my hand in.

"Oh." I couldn't think of anything else to say. I stood up. "Well, I just stopped by to tell you he was back."

Laura stopped swimming and treaded water.

"I didn't do anything with Michael, y'know."

"I know. I was being a loser. It was just Joel and everything. Was it you who told about Joel seeing the shrink?"

"I didn't mean to. It sort of came out when I was talking to Minnie Kazmaier and she blabbed it. I'm really sorry."

"I know."

She started swimming again.
"You wanna come in?"
"I don't have a suit."
"Get my green one. No, it's got a hole in it, get another one. Whatever. The door's unlocked."

CHAPTER 26

JOEL CAME DOWN FROM THE ATTIC THE NEXT MORNING. He didn't really want to, Mom asked him to. She made him some sandwiches and he ate them. It wasn't much. No one talked or anything, but it was a start. Later when I was in my room listening to music, Joel came in and sat at my desk.

"You remember that fight at school with Kyle Kroeger?"

"Yeah." Like I was going to forget.

"Well, I wanted to kill him. I tried to kick him in the head. If Michael hadn't stopped me, I'd have kicked him right in the head with my boots."

"I know. I get really mad like that sometimes too."

I think he was there because he was bored or lonely and realized you eventually have to carry on with your life, even if you're just back from running away and you've just found out your parents aren't your parents. Anyway, I didn't care why. I had been really missing him.

The last weekend before school was starting, Mom invited some of our friends over for dinner – Michael, Laura and VJ. She made chicken breasts, mashed potatoes, asparagus and fresh buns. And banana cake. She also made pizza, in case someone didn't like the food, but everyone did.

Joel would have helped the situation at the dinner table if he'd been a bit more lively. He was trying, but he'd been very quiet ever since he got back. I think he felt like everyone was staring at him and watching him, which they were.

Things got better after dessert when we went up to the attic. Laura and VJ were very excited, giddy almost, and wanted to hear about Joel's northern adventure. Michael seemed restless. He was walking around, picking things up, putting things down, pacing. Only he's tall and the ceiling is sloped, so it was sort of stooped pacing. When he saw me watching him, he mouthed, "Let's go."

I told the others we were going down to catch some air, then led him downstairs and out into the backyard. Mom and Dad were in the living room and I didn't think they saw or heard us, but to be safe we went to the west side of the shed, which can't be seen from the attic window or anywhere else in the house.

He stood there with his hands in his pockets, as though I was the one that had initiated the little outing, so I said, "What?"

He asked, "What's been goin' on?"

"What do you mean?"

"Why have you been acting funny?"

This conversation could have gone on forever like that. Me saying, "acting like what?" and him saying, "you know" and me saying, "no, I don't." I didn't have the energy for it, so I decided to cut through the garbage.

"You'll have to be more direct. Just say whatever it is that's on your mind."

He looked a bit surprised. "Okay, why did you walk out on me at the pool that day? I looked like an idiot in front of everyone, standing there shouting, 'Roxanne, Roxanne.'"

"I didn't hear you. Well, maybe I heard someone calling, but I didn't know it was you. Anyway, I thought you were with Dawn."

"As if I'd be with Dawn."

"She was jumping on your back and everything. Trying to duck you under."

"You know Dawn. She needs a lot of attention. It's best to give it to her or she won't go away ever. She clings."

I knew what he was talking about. I'd been there.

"I thought you would have come over or called me or something."

"I wanted to, but I figured you'd think it was loser of me to hang around when your family was going through all that."

"Yeah, I guess," I said.

That's when he said the thing I can't remember now, something like, "I guess if we're going to make this work, we'll have to blah, blah, blah." I don't remember anything that came after that, because he definitely said "make this work," which meant he and I were a number, an item, as my mother calls it. I stopped listening to what he was saying and instead started planning what we would name our horses and whether our acreage would be on the north edge of the city or the south. Then I realized he was waiting for me to say something, answer a question.

I had no idea what the question was, so I smiled my most charming smile and said, "Did you ask me something?"

He laughed and said, "Never mind."

He put his arm around me. We stood there looking up at the sky through the trees and it reminded me of the night we snuck down to the bridges. The moon was peeking through the branches in the same way and the wind was gently turning the leaves over and back again, like children who couldn't quite get comfortable enough to fall asleep.

"You cold?" he asked.

"No. You?"

"No."

"I guess we should go in," I said. "They'll make fun of us. And Joel might give you that look again."

Michael leaned over and kissed me.

I remember I could smell the pines. And that his shirt felt cool on my fingers.

I'd kissed guys before, playing Spin the Bottle and stuff, but those kisses didn't feel like this. Like a buzz saw, like electricity. It lasted maybe three seconds and I had about an hour's worth of thoughts in those three seconds. I thought about how young we were, and how hard it was going to be to stay together until we're old enough to really have a chance to stay together. My brain was chanting, "Oh please don't let this end, please let him love me like this forever. Please don't let me be only thirteen, let the years fly by, oh please, God, until we're eighteen and this can be for real."

But then I told myself not to think about the future, not to think too much at all, like Grandma said. Just live in the moment.

When we went in, everyone was downstairs, talking and laughing and sort of milling around eating the cake crumbs and stuff. Laura was on the phone to her mother, asking her if we could come over for a swim, to which her mother said yes and our parents said yes too.

Michael and VJ borrowed suits from Joel, we got in the van and Dad let Joel drive. None of the others had their learner's yet.

What a good night. What a peaceful, incredible night.

I sat at the edge of the pool while Laura and VJ got a fire happening in the pit and Joel and Michael swam back and forth, slowly. I sat there, looking at them and thinking about how much I loved them both. Michael was telling Joel how worried he was when he disappeared. Joel was telling him about how awful it was and how lonely he felt when Curtis died. Michael said Curtis had lived a decent life. Joel said he planned to keep seeing the shrink, but he didn't want the whole world to know. Michael said, "Yeah, people are funny about that kind of stuff." Then they talked about basketball. I felt some bad feelings lift off my head and float away into the air.

Laura and VJ came over and jumped in the pool, splashing me, and Laura asked, "What were you guys doing behind the shed earlier?"

We had a good time.

So, that was August.

September

CHAPTER 27

EVERY DAY, THINGS GET A BIT BETTER. IT WAS ALL WEIRD, it still is. Mom and Dad and Uncle Lee are trying to love us without driving us crazy and we're sort of trying too.

School is starting tomorrow. I've been outlining some plans for getting through the next year. Things I believe I should work on. I'm going to try to live in the present, not to worry about what will happen tomorrow and how I'll deal with it when it does. I'll try to stay active, like Grandma says. Let's see, what else ...

1. Learn to cook some gourmet dishes.
2. Try to get a job out at the stables so I can be around the horses more.
3. Work harder on the sciences.
4. Work on lay-ups.
5. Find Joel a new girlfriend. Maybe.
6. Be happier all the time, not just with Michael.
7. Be a good person, not get involved in the back-stabbing at school.
8. Try to get Uncle Lee to relax.
9. Kill any female that looks at Michael.

This morning, Dad gave Mom a tree, a little Japanese bonsai.

"What's this?"

"It's a 'You're-My-Wife' present."

My father is a mysterious man. Maybe he isn't as strong as I always used to believe. Maybe I even love him more for that.

I dropped by Mrs. Verdecchio's house today. I gave her a paper I'd written about names and their meanings and how different people in the world choose names and about how everything has a name, even if we don't know what to call it. She invited me in for tea.

I am a girl, I am thirteen, I am a person who has an excellent boyfriend.

The stars have all moved. Orion is in a different place tonight than he was earlier this summer. And it's okay with me that the stars are what they are.

I've moved too.

I used to think of the universe as a thing that hangs static in the sky, like a photograph, but that was when I was very young and the stars had color. Now I know the earth whirls and so does everything else. It's like a dance that looks complicated the first time you see it, but isn't. Everything knows where it's supposed to go next.

I've learned one thing that's true this summer, which I'll try not to forget. Things can change and you can think you're lost. But you can find your way again. You can still end up where you're supposed to be.

September.